Morgan BLUESTONE

Tom Claffey

TREATY OAK PUBLISHERS

PUBLISHER'S NOTE

This is a work of fiction. None of the characters, business establishments, or events is based on actual people, living or dead, or their lives or circumstances. All material is a product of the author's imagination. Any resemblance to actual people, businesses, or events is just a coincidence and purely unintentional.

Printed and published in the United States of America

TREATY OAK PUBLISHERS

ISBN-10: 1-943658-21-8
ISBN-13: 978-1-943658-21-3

ACKNOWLEDGMENTS

Very special thanks to:

Elizabeth Bauer, MS, DVM, Program Director, Front Range Community College, Colorado

Laura Brodie, PhD, Professor of English, Washington and Lee University, Virginia

JoAnne Bitsui, Cottonwood Springs, Arizona

Jasmine Blackwater, Monument Valley High School, Class of 2013, Kayenta, Arizona

Germaine Daye, DVM, Director, NTC Veterinary Teaching Hospital, Crownpoint, New Mexico

Bruce V. Hofkin, PhD, Department of Biology, University of New Mexico

Racheal Holiday, Monument Valley High School, Class of 2013, Kayenta, Arizona

Britt Levy, University of Pennsylvania School of Veterinary Medicine

Eva Lipton-Ormond, UNM Taos Summer Writers' Conference

Clyde McBride, CTE Coordinator, Monument Valley High School, Kayenta, Arizona

Dell Rae Moellenberg, Colorado State University

Theodore C. Price, DVM, Past Chairman, New Mexico Board of Veterinary Medicine

Summer Wood, UNM Taos Summer Writers' Conference

My deepest gratitude to **Dean A. Hendrickson**, DVM, MS, Director and Professor, Colorado State University Veterinary Teaching Hospital, for his generously sharing with me his time and his profound knowledge of veterinary medicine.

* * *

CTE	Career Technical Education	NTC	Navajo Technical College
DVM	Doctor of Veterinary Medicine	PhD	Doctor of Philosophy
MS	Master of Science	UNM	University of New Mexico

ALSO BY TOM CLAFFEY

ELEVEN TO ONE

DUBHE

LADIES AND GENTLEMEN OF THE JURY

AND THE ANGELS CRIED

8-BALL, CORNER POCKET

HOOT 'N' HOLLER

SEARCHING FOR C.W. McCALL

BLOOMFIELD TO BAGHDAD

103rd MERIDIAN

To
Cynthia Stone

If you talk to the animals they will talk with you and you will know each other.

Chief Dan George (1899-1981)
Squamish Band, Salish Indian Tribe
Burrard Inlet, British Columbia

Morgan
BLUESTONE

SHIWANA

Chapter 1

The thunder. Like nothing she had ever heard. Morgan Bluestone stood alone in a sea of a million buffalo, stretching from one horizon to the other. They appeared, in the beginning, as black dots near the edge of a thick grass-green wooly carpet. The stampede was deafening, a reverberating roar that deadened her senses. They were all around her, rampaging westward, sweeping her off the lush prairie grass, their shrouded black eyes beckoning her to become one of them.

She was dripping in sweat but sensed no fear as she reached up and pulled herself aboard one of the bulls. She pressed her body against his humped shoulders and leaned down to grip the horns on his shaggy-haired head. His heavy breathing siphoned the air around them as he ran and she inhaled the earthy hot aroma of his chocolate brown mane. No longer able to hold on, she tumbled in slow motion over his head. Thundering, pounding hooves hammered the grasslands. Then she rose, lifted above the stampede by some mysterious force.

Morgan awoke, clutching the black and white blanket beneath her chin. Her hand trembled as she reached for the clock beside her bed. 4:30 AM. Hands-on procedures and evaluations in the Critical Care Unit would begin in three and a-half hours. She was in her third year at Colorado State University College of Veterinary Medicine. She rolled over.

What was the dream all about? Did it have anything to do with the buffalo herd she and her roommate, Suki Winters, assisted in transporting to Montana? The dangers they faced from some of the local cattle ranchers? Dangers, born by the cruelty and greed of a few? Would her career in veterinary medicine bring her face-to-face with similar conflicts? If so, she welcomed them.

She climbed out of her narrow single bed and sat on its edge for a few moments. Then she walked to the window. A gentle breeze tugged at the blinds. She raised them and looked down at the damp early morning grass. Except for the streetlights and stars, it was dark.

An instant later, she spotted movement beside a large aspen tree forty yards away. She squinted and leaned forward. A buffalo calf with reddish tan hair grazed a short distance from the apartment building. It may have escaped from one of the holding pens at the nearby Veterinary Teaching Hospital. Although, during her childhood, she had also overheard stories about ghosts and mysterious sightings of animals.

The calf stopped and gazed up at her while it continued chewing. She noticed a patch of white fur, three or four inches in diameter, beneath its left eye. She retrieved her glasses and opened the window to search the area for the calf's mother. She scanned the shrubbery and trees and found no sign of mom. The only sounds were from light traffic on Drake Road, a half-block away. A few tree branches swayed in the light breeze and the buffalo calf, chewing with deliberation, kept its eyes focused on her.

Morgan turned and grabbed a coat from the closet. Careful not to awaken Suki, she threw it over her pajamas and ran downstairs. She opened the front door of the small apartment building and looked to the spot where the calf had stood. Nothing. In the foliage beside the door, a cricket chirped three times. From somewhere near the aspen where the calf had been grazing, another cricket answered. The early morning light changed structures and trees into silhouettes.

The door closed behind her and Morgan plodded across the open area to a spot beneath the aspen. She stopped a few feet from its trunk and looked down, wishing she had brought a flashlight. Hoof prints appeared in the grass where it was eaten down close to soil level. And a smell. Like the smell she remembered from Ted Turner's Vermejo Park Ranch, where she and several classmates visited his buffalo herd. She knelt on the ground and ran her hands across the surface. The grass was almost warm, like the calf had just left, and was close by watching her.

She continued scanning the immediate area while moisture seeped from the grass into the fabric of her pajamas. Except for the subdued glow and reflection from streetlights, the neighborhood was dark. Anyone else might have been afraid, out here by herself, but Morgan was not. Somewhere close by was the buffalo calf. When she was a child, she and her grandfather sometimes spoke of the strength and spiritual bonding one feels in the presence of buffalo.

She inhaled, let her breath out, and then straightened up and walked back to her room.

* * *

A short distance away, shielded by a mulberry hedge, the young buffalo watched Morgan. Then he turned and faded into the quiet glow of dawn.

* * *

After a quick bowl of cereal and cup of coffee, Morgan and Suki left their apartment and walked the few blocks to the Veterinary Teaching Hospital. On a wall in the reception area of the main entrance hung a huge bronze casting of Bart the Bear's paw print. Bart the Bear, a former patient at the hospital, and star of Legends of the Fall, stood nine and one-half feet tall and weighed 1,500 pounds.

Sometimes, before taking a test, Suki walked to the reception area, kissed the tips of her fingers, and patted Bart's paw print. Then she rushed to the exam room. Today, running late, she raced through the building entrance and sent a wink with an air kiss at the paw, hoping Bart would understand.

* * *

Morgan stood over a scrub sink in the Critical Care Unit, thinking about the buffalo calf. It was midmorning. Had the calf and his mother, in fact, somehow gotten out of one of the vet school holding pens? Or was it a vision?

Jimmy Castle, a fellow student, scrubbed at the adjacent sink. Jimmy was from Grand Junction, Colorado, where his dad had a veterinary clinic. He was a shy, friendly guy and Morgan enjoyed his smile and his energy. He sported short sandy-colored hair. "You sure are deep in thought, Morgan."

"Guess I am, Jimmy." She rubbed her cheek against her sleeve. "It shows, huh?"

"Anything I can help you with?" He rinsed the soap off his hands and arms. Jimmy stood just under six feet tall with the lithe, athletic build of a tennis player.

"No." She grabbed a towel and began drying her hands. "I was thinking about a buffalo calf I saw early this morning from my apartment window."

"I heard someone in the Bovine Herd class last week mention they saw a loose buffalo calf around here. A good-looking animal."

"Do you remember where they spotted it?"

"Just off-campus; over in your neighborhood, I think. Near Redwing Road and Flicker." He turned. "Maybe he's looking out for you, Morgan. Maybe your guardian angel is a young buffalo."

"I would like that."

Morgan walked toward the examining room and Jimmy followed. Three other students and Professor of Surgery, Dr. Erik Bourland, joined them. Morgan had spent enough time with him to appreciate Bourland as a laid-back family man who enjoyed talking about his five kids.

On the stainless steel table lay an anesthetized female German shepherd. She had been struck by a car on Highway 287, not far from the CSU campus. Her lower jaw was open and her pink tongue draped from her mouth. The dog's breathing came slow and shallow, her chest rising and falling in an even rhythm. Her left rear leg had been X-rayed in ER after one of the nurses removed the gauze and tape that had been wrapped around a crude splint at the accident scene.

Morgan placed her hand on the shepherd's neck area, submerging her fingers in its soft brown hair.

"Miss Bluestone?" Dr. Bourland said.

"Yes, Doctor."

He pointed to the x-ray light box viewer positioned against the white cinder block wall. "Tell us what we are looking at in the x-ray and how you are going to treat it."

Morgan glanced at the viewer, her hand still resting on the

German shepherd.

"Because you are going to treat the injured dog." He nodded to her. "This is your show."

Morgan fixed her eyes on the shepherd, then walked to the x-ray. With a slight tremor in her hand, she put on her horn-rimmed glasses. Her eyes narrowed as she studied the image of the dog's leg. She drew a pen from the pocket on her left sleeve and, without touching the x-ray, traced a line where she detected a simple fracture.

She glanced down at the shepherd, then back at the screen. "This doesn't seem to be as critical as I had suspected."

"Tell us what you see," Bourland said.

"A simple fracture of the metatarsus, mid-way between the tarsus and the phalange, about two inches above her paw." Morgan turned to the doctor. "She is a relatively young dog. She can heal quickly."

"And what else?"

Morgan hesitated as she shifted her weight from one foot to the other. "I see no need for surgery and would recommend splinting or a lightweight fiberglass cast."

"Okay." He nodded. "Which one?"

"She is likely still pretty active." Morgan returned the pen to her pocket and looked at the other four students. "A fiberglass cast is what I recommend."

Britt Jennison, a former veterinary technician from Philadelphia, was one of the four other students. Her light brown hair shone beneath the exam room overhead lights. She nodded at Morgan with a twinkle in her eye.

"Good job, Bluestone. She's your patient. You take it from here." He turned to the other students. "We'll reconvene here tomorrow morning and Miss Bluestone will brief us on what she has done in the interim. After that we will proceed to the Equine Hospital. Then—"

"Doctor?" Jimmy Castle raised his hand.

"Yes."

"I'd like to remain here and assist Morgan with the casting procedure."

Dr. Bourland turned to Morgan. "Is that okay with you?"

"Yes, Doctor."

"I will expect the best from both of you." He ran his fingers through his hair. "As you all know, this is foaling season, the season when baby horses arrive with wobbly legs and empty stomachs."

The students nodded.

"Foaling season usually runs from February through April or May." He paused. "During the remainder of this week, we will be on the other side of the building at the Equine Hospital, applying what you have been studying diligently. We will apply that knowledge to hands-on theriogenology, animal reproduction, and the associated birthing problems. Which are?"

"Dystocias," a student standing beside him said.

Bourland turned. The student was Jason Strandberg, a freckled, red-headed farm boy from Durango, Colorado. "That is correct. Very good, Strandberg." He looked down at the sedated German shepherd. "Bluestone and Castle, you have work to do." He nodded to the students. "I will see all of you tomorrow."

After the others had left, Morgan and Jimmy, with the examining room nurse, set about casting the shepherd's rear leg. Jimmy Castle and the nurse, without hesitation, followed Morgan's instructions. Inside of an hour, the procedure was completed and the dog awakened from her deep sleep.

Later, Morgan went to the wire-enclosed recovery pen where

she sat on the floor with the dog, gently stroking her head.

After retrieving his backpack and books, Jimmy followed and sat beside her. "You're going to be a good veterinarian, Morgan. I've never seen such concern for an animal."

The dog stirred.

"I adore animals. They give so much, and ask for so little." She stroked the dog's head. "Want to come with me to the livestock pens when we leave here?"

"Sure. What for?"

"To see if we might find a mother buffalo and her calf."

"What's special about the calf? You mentioned it earlier, while we were scrubbing."

"I'm not sure." She stroked the shepherd's head. "I had a dream last night about a herd of buffalo. A huge herd. My grandfather used to talk about buffalo herds." She paused. "Maybe there is something in my blood. In my DNA. Something is pulling on me, Jimmy. I feel myself reaching out. Reaching back. That little calf this morning… the way he looked at me. Like he recognized me. Like he was asking me for help or something."

She looked up at Jimmy's face. "I can't explain it."

He touched her arm. "There is no need to explain, Morgan."

Chapter 2

. . . Walking on shore this evening I met with a buffaloe calf which attached itself to me and continued to follow close at my heels until I embarked and left it.

Meriwether Lewis
April 22, 1805

* * *

Barney Reid was in charge of the barn staff at the Veterinary Teaching Hospital on Drake Road. A tall cowboy with skin like bronzed leather, he reminded Morgan of her uncle Shonto, a favorite among her mother's brothers. Barney put in long hours and loved being around the animals and the student veterinarians. He could have easily become a vet himself, but he didn't have the desire to tackle the hard academic grind of vet school. He was an unassuming guy, known to work harder than anyone else around him. And the crow's feet beside his eyes forewarned a ready laugh.

Morgan and Jimmy stood on either side of him as they waited outside the holding pen. "See that mama buffalo there in the back?" he said. "The one staring at us?"

"Yes," Morgan said. Her hands were stuffed in the back

pockets of her worn jeans. Dust coated her cowboy boots.

"She and her calf somehow got out last night. They did it once before." He chuckled. "The night staff called me at home. We found 'em over close to that ditch on Redwing Road early this morning."

"I thought I saw the calf when I got up this morning," Morgan said, relief in her voice. "But I wasn't entirely certain. That's why I asked Jimmy to come over here with me, to see if he was here. He's a cute little guy."

Barney turned. "Where was that? What time?"

"I live in an apartment in that neighborhood." She glanced to her right across Drake Road. "Around four-thirty. Wasn't it difficult bringing them back here to the holding pen?"

"Someone drove me over there and I walked back. They followed me."

"The mama and the calf followed you across Drake Road?"

"There were just a few cars and pickups at that hour."

"That's surprising." Morgan looked up at Barney.

"What's surprising? That the traffic stopped?"

"No," she laughed, "that the mama and calf followed you." Morgan glanced at the small herd. "How do you suppose the calf got that patch of white hair beneath his left eye?"

"Probably ran into something or got kicked. That white patch happened because he lost the pigment capacity in the hair follicles." He lifted his cowboy hat and scratched his head. "I've got work to do. Be careful."

Morgan walked into the corral, a large holding pen where five buffalo cows were gathered with their calves. Jimmy Castle shuffled along behind her, his shirttail hanging out one side of his jeans.

Morgan's nostrils filled with that same distinctive bovine

smell she had noticed when she knelt on the ground outside her dorm. She surveyed the expanse between herself and the animals at the rear of the pen and remembered Barney's caution about the protective buffalo mama cows. "They don't like us to get too close to their calves," he had said. "And they can be mean as hell."

Morgan stopped near the center of the pen.

"What are you thinking, Morgan?" Jimmy said.

"That I don't want to get any closer." She studied the small herd. "I don't want to scare them."

Just then, the calf with the white patch stuck its head out from behind his mother. He looked at Morgan for several moments, then walked toward her. A few steps in front of his mother, he stopped and raised his nose as though confirming her scent. He was an inquisitive youngster with knobby front knees and a shiny black nose. Above his ears, near the top of his head, protruded small gray nubs—buffalo horns in their infancy.

Morgan stood motionless, studying his face and the white spot of hair. She extended her hand. With eyes more watchful, the calf walked toward her and stopped again.

"Come on, boy," she whispered. "Come on."

The calf took a few tentative steps and paused to sniff the air again. Then a few more.

Morgan felt an almost electrifying sensation when the calf's nose touched the ends of her fingers. He extended his tongue and licked her hand, all the while his mother observed from a distance. Morgan sensed the mama buffalo's readiness to spring, to challenge anyone or anything that might threaten her calf. Sweat beaded on her forehead and gravity pulled a rivulet down the side of her nose.

Jimmy Castle stood motionless observing the drama.

The calf playfully shook his head from side to side. Then, keeping his eyes on Morgan, he took two steps back. His mother watched their every move, staring at them but not interfering. The calf spread his front legs and lowered his head.

"Are you inviting me to play?" Morgan said. She retrieved one of the three or four sugar cubes she usually carried in her pocket for horses or mules she might encounter and placed it on the tip of her fingers toward the buffalo calf. "I am going to call you Shiwana."

The calf studied her extended fingers holding the sugar cube. He grunted.

"Come, Shiwana. Come."

The mother buffalo kept her gaze fixed on Morgan.

"I'll give you this sugar cube, my little friend. Then Jimmy and I will leave."

The calf edged a step forward and took the cube with his pink tongue. Morgan lowered her hand to her side. Then she retreated to stand beside Jimmy.

"What does Shiwana mean?" he said.

"The Shiwana are cloud spirits who live in the sky. Very often they protect us." She turned back to the calf. "That white patch of fur beneath his eye looks like a little cloud, don't you think?"

"Yes. Yes, it does." Jimmy reached down and took her hand. His face turned pink.

Morgan sensed his hand tighten on hers. She glanced at him and smiled.

They stepped back and closed the gate to the holding pen, then took the path to the Veterinary Training Hospital. "Morgan?"

"Yes."

He stopped and faced her. "When we graduate and become licensed… would you consider practicing in Grand Junction?"

"What do you mean?"

"My father wants to retire from his veterinary practice. And sell his clinic."

"And?"

"You and I could set up a partnership and take over the practice. I'm sure Dad would sell it at a reasonable price."

Morgan furrowed her brow. "You're serious, aren't you?"

"Very serious."

She smiled, then continued toward the hospital building.

"I think you and I would be a great partnership."

"I do, too, Jimmy. And I'm flattered by your invitation to join you at your father's clinic. But—"

"But what?" He stumbled on a loose stone, then regained his balance.

Morgan stopped and stared across at the vacant pasture beside the hospital. "If it were not for my family, my people, and my friends, I would not be here at Colorado State working to become a vet." She placed her hands in the back pockets of her jeans. "Many times I miss the land, the culture, the tradition… the animals."

"I don't understand."

"I am here, Jimmy, with you and the other members of our class because of who I am. A hard-working student who has been able to learn and make the grades we must, in order to remain and graduate with a degree of Doctor of Veterinary Medicine. I am also here because of what I am. A Native American. A member of The Navajo Nation for whom a door has been opened so that I will one day return to the reservation to serve my people. No law says I cannot be your partner in practice in Grand Junction. But this is a commitment I cannot break. A commitment I have made to my people and to myself to graduate and serve them."

A certain firmness came through her voice. "I have been away for eight years. Studying harder than I have ever studied in my life. This morning in the examining room, for a moment I wasn't sure of myself. I wasn't confident I could properly diagnose and treat the German shepherd."

Jimmy frowned. "You seemed confident."

She shook her head and glanced to her left. The buffalo calf stood in the holding pen watching her.

Jimmy hesitated, then he reached for the door.

His offer was tempting. Morgan imagined herself settled in Grand Junction with an already thriving practice. An easy choice. But also, a choice that would betray a commitment. She sighed and walked through the door Jimmy held open to the veterinary building.

Chapter 3

Turquoise is a token of well-being brought to us by the Holy People.

JoAnne Bitsui
Navajo Nation
Cottonwood Springs, Arizona

* * *

Near Kewa Pueblo, north of Albuquerque, were mines of blue stone or sky stone which today is called turquoise.

Morgan was raised in Kewa Pueblo by her mother, Cynthia, and her grandmother, Maria. She never knew her father, Jonathan Bluestone, a tribal policeman who was killed three weeks before she was born by a drunken driver behind the wheel of a black Chevy Blazer. On the rare occasions when her grandmother spoke of that night and of the people who came to their home, Morgan visualized them talking in the kitchen and sometimes imagined herself in her mother's womb, feeling her sobs.

Cynthia was a stunning woman with bright brown eyes and long gray hair, often tied behind her head. Maria, her father's mother, grew up in Shiprock, New Mexico, on the Navajo

(Dinè) Reservation. Morgan called her *Nalí*, the Navajo word for grandmother.

When Morgan left their adobe home to begin her freshman year at the University of New Mexico, Cynthia, now a nurse with the Indian Health Service, hugged her tightly

Her grandmother, Maria, waited her turn. She held out both of her hands to grasp Morgan's. "Your journey from here to the University is but a few miles, but it is only the beginning of a much longer journey. One which truly cannot be measured." She wiped away a tear. "Your mother was the first in our family to go to college. And now you are the second. I am proud of you, my child. And I will miss you."

Morgan wrapped her arms around her grandmother who it seemed had in that instant become smaller. She leaned down and held her close. "I will miss you, Nali. More than you know."

* * *

Driving east on Central Avenue, she turned left at Stanford to the UNM campus. Ahead was a multi-level parking structure, similar to structures she had navigated in downtown Albuquerque. Only this one looked different and felt different. She was swimming into unknown waters.

"Get a grip, girl," she muttered to herself. She erased the intimidation from her mind and eased the tired and rusted green GMC pickup to an empty space on the second level. Soon she was walking down paths, some narrow, some wide, between and around buildings with few names and numbers.

The faces of other students appeared to be focused on universes within themselves. She passed many white faces, a few Hispanic faces, and fewer Native American faces, but none of them made eye contact. Disoriented and looking around, Morgan felt alone and adrift. The Indian School campus in Santa Fe was big, but the people were friendly. This campus at UNM was immense. "Holy crap!" she muttered. "I am lost. Totally lost."

She eased toward a low wall surrounding a cottonwood tree, then sat on its cold cement surface and dropped her backpack on the sidewalk beneath her legs. She bit her lower lip and unzipped the side pocket on the pack and reached for the note pad with the name of her advisor and his room number.

"May I join you?"

Morgan looked up, shading her eyes with her hand, at a girl her age with straight black hair and bright blue eyes. "Sure," she said with shyness in her voice, "have a seat." She nodded to her left.

The girl sat on the low wall and set a notebook and two textbooks on the ledge between them. Then she turned. "My name's Suki Winters."

"Morgan Bluestone."

Suki was quiet. She rubbed the palms of her hands together. "You from around here?"

Morgan nodded. "Kewa Pueblo. North of Albuquerque. Between here and Santa Fe. How about you?"

"Bozeman, Montana." Suki Winters' blue eyes danced when she spoke.

"Are you a freshman?"

"Yeah. Biology, pre-vet."

Morgan brightened. "I am, too. Only I'm lost. I don't know where I am. This campus is so big. And the people…"

"I got here yesterday and felt the same way, but you know what?"

"What?"

"I remembered having the same experience going from junior high to high school in Bozeman." Suki smiled. "We'll get used to it, Morgan."

"Promise?"

"I promise."

Morgan breathed deeply and let it out. Then she laughed. "Thank you. I needed that."

"You're welcome. You said you were lost. What are you looking for?" Suki said.

"Castetter Hall, the Department of Biology. I have no idea where it is." She pulled a campus map from her green and blue backpack.

"You won't need that map." Suki pointed to a tan colored building on the other side of the large courtyard area. "I just came from Castetter Hall. Met with my advisor and got signed up." She displayed a sassy dimple on her left cheek. It went well with her impish grin. "Let me walk you over there."

* * *

During the next four years, Suki spent so many weekends at Morgan's Kewa Pueblo home, Cynthia Bluestone called Suki her second daughter.

Following their sophomore and junior years, they became hired hands on Suki's family farm in Bozeman. One of those summer visits found them working temporarily as research assistants on a project to transfer a herd of wild buffalo from Yellowstone National Park to the Fort Peck Indian Reservation in northeastern Montana.

The nine-hour journey in the convoy of three Freightliner

18-wheelers was strenuous and tiring for the buffalo, for the drivers, and for Morgan and Suki. Their welcoming reception at the reservation was one Morgan would never forget. The Montana Governor and the Assiniboine and Sioux tribal leaders were among those welcoming the convoy and its cargo. Before he left to return to the state capitol in Helena, the governor personally thanked and shook hands with them. "You two pre-vet students from the University of New Mexico make us all proud."

After all of the animals had been unloaded into temporary holding pens, Morgan and Suki entered one of the pens to assist in their feeding and watering. Later, as they prepared to leave, one of the calves trotted up behind Morgan and nudged her for more hay. The calf's mother stood at a distance, her eyes locked on Morgan.

Morgan laughed and reached for a fistful of hay. She handed it to the calf. "Here you are, my little friend." She patted the top of his reddish-brown head and she and Suki continued to the holding pen entrance.

They were closing the metal gate when a Sioux tribal elder with chiseled face lines approached them. He took their hands in his. "The arrival of these buffalo has deep spiritual meaning for us."

Morgan's clothes and Suki's were covered with dirt from the corral and they were sweating. Morgan knew they smelled like the buffalo they just delivered.

The proud elder's long gray hair dropped behind his shoulders. He tightened his grip on their hands. "Thank you," he said. "My name is Teetonka. Teetonka means 'Talks too much.'" He laughed.

Morgan laughed with him. "We are honored. It is we who

should thank you."

"What is your tribe?"

"Kewa Pueblo. In New Mexico."

"This is wonderful to witness," Suki said, "to see your immediate kinship. A Kewa girl and a Sioux tribal elder, no less. How cool!"

"Our tribes and our people welcome you both to our land," he said. "You have travelled a great distance from Yellowstone."

"Almost 500 miles. It will take a few days for the buffalo to recover."

"Did all of the buffalo survive the trip?"

"One of them died," Suki said. "A yearling."

"I will pray to the spirits for the yearling and," he said with a smile, "I will also pray to the spirits for sending both of you to be with us." He turned to Suki. "And who are your people?"

Morgan spoke first. "Suki is my sister."

Teetonka nodded. "I understand."

Suki beamed as Teetonka reached to her face and removed a blade of pasture grass from her chin. "Welcome, my Kewa sisters."

* * *

A Billings newspaper carried a story of the meeting between the two young women and the Sioux elder, along with a photograph of the elder embracing both girls. In an adjacent column, a Montana state senator criticized the presence of what he termed "two out-of-state agitators."

The following day, as Morgan and Suki said goodbye to the drivers of the 18-wheelers who would return to their home base, a small group of protesters shouted obscenities and told them

to go back home to New Mexico. Some carried signs condemn-
ing the arrival of buffalo on ranges where only cattle should be
allowed to graze.

One of the protesters was a teenager wearing a beat-up cowboy hat, a gray duster, and thick glasses. He stood inches from
Suki, cursing her, with clenched fists at his side.

The newspaper account of this confrontation included a
picture of "Suki Winters, a resident of Bozeman," flipping a
bird in the teenager's face. "I may be a student at University of
New Mexico," she said, "but I am also a resident of Montana.
So screw you!"

When asked to comment on Miss Winters' statement,
Morgan Bluestone threw an arm across Suki Winters' shoulder
and grinned. "Not much I can add to that, is there?"

When he was later contacted by a wire service and asked to
say something of the incident, the UNM biology professor and
student advisor for Miss Winters and Miss Bluestone chuckled.
"Vet students are a tough bunch, regardless of where they go to
school—New Mexico, Montana, Colorado." Morgan and Suki
happened to be in his office at the time, dropping off their report of the trip. Still holding the phone, the professor winked at
them and added, "I'm kinda proud of these two young ladies."

* * *

Morgan felt a spiritual covenant with the Yellowstone buffalo
herd and the Sioux elder. She and the wise Teetonka, of different
tribes and nations, bonded in that wide northeastern Montana
pasture with a mutual dream—the reunion of brothers and
sisters and the sacred bison. She smiled at the memory of the

buffalo calf walking up behind her to snatch hay from her hand.

And she sensed that one day she and Suki would return. To this place and the buffalo herd.

Chapter 4

The following spring, still at UNM, Morgan and Suki enrolled in BIOL 435, Animal Physiology, to study the function of organ systems in animals. Though the class was large, she found the professor an affable, easy-to-know man in his mid-forties. Dr. Timothy Garcia also held an undergraduate degree in American History.

One class, in particular, stuck in Morgan's mind, because it dealt with two large animals she wanted to learn more about: the horse and the buffalo. She reviewed her notes from that lecture and transcribed them into a single summary:

Hernando Cortes brought a few horses from Spain to the Americas in 1519. In Mexico, these horses multiplied. 200 years and many miles later, there were thousands of horses.

The Pueblo Indians of the current US were probably the first Indian horsemen. The Navajo tribe was next and then the Sioux.

Also on the vast plains were nearly 50 million buffalo (bison). Buffalo and bison are the same. On horseback, Indians hunted buffalo more easily than they had in the past.

This period ended when cavalry, railroads, and hide hunters destroyed the buffalo. Only a few, concealed in Yellowstone, were spared.

* * *

Time passed quickly for Morgan and Suki. Examinations were taken and examinations passed. Each received a Bachelor's Degree in Biology and they both applied to the freshman class at Colorado State University College of Veterinary Medicine and Biomedical Sciences in Fort Collins.

The day the reply letter from Colorado State arrived at their home and the excitement she, her mother, and her grandmother shared when she opened the letter was one Morgan would always remember.

Her grandmother received the letter, addressed to Morgan, and placed it unopened at the center of the dining room table. Cynthia picked up the envelope when she arrived home in the late afternoon and returned it to the table.

"What do you think the letter says?" Maria said.

"I pray it is Morgan's letter of acceptance to the Veterinary School."

Maria folded her arms across her chest. "So do I, my daughter. So do I."

Then they and the unopened envelope waited for two more hours. When Morgan arrived home and saw it, she dashed to the table and tore it open. A smile burst across her face and she let out a squeal. She had been accepted in the forthcoming freshman class.

As the three women shared their moment of joy the telephone rang. Morgan picked it up. It was Suki, calling from Bozeman.

Cynthia and Maria turned away smiling as Morgan and Suki noisily celebrated their achievement.

* * *

In Bozeman, Montana, Jack Winters opened a bottle of Jack Daniel's Single Barrel Whiskey. "We're damned proud of you, Suki," he toasted, as he, his wife Maude, and Suki tapped their glasses above the dining room table.

* * *

The morning Morgan was ready to leave home with her belongings tied down in a newly acquired used Ford F-150 pickup, her grandmother took her hands. She wore her traditional Navajo dress of broomstick skirt, velvet blouse, and moccasins. "May the spirits be with you, child."

Then she looked down at her wrist and removed her cherished turquoise and silver bracelet and placed it around Morgan's. Its center stone, the size of a silver dollar, was deep sky blue. On either side were smaller stones of the same deep color. The silver holding the turquoise stones was worn and rounded from decades of wear.

Morgan embraced Maria. "I will miss you, Nalí. Someday I would like to live where you lived when you were given this bracelet—in Shiprock with the Dinè."

"Perhaps someday you will, child." She laughed and her tummy bounced beneath her skirt. "May I come with you?"

A few minutes later, Morgan looked in the rearview mirror of the truck and saw her mother and grandmother waving. Through clouded eyes and with a lump in her throat, she lowered the window and returned the wave. She had one more stop to make. One more goodbye.

* * *

Morgan had good reason to prize her friendship with the Albuquerque internist. After her father was killed, Doctor James C. Morgan, an energetic man, six feet tall and 175 pounds with thinning gray hair, took Cynthia under his wing as his nursing assistant and, at Morgan's birth, visited with his banker and established a college fund for her. Choosing a name for her infant daughter was not difficult for Cynthia. She named her Morgan.

Doc Morgan sold his medical practice when he was in his mid-fifties to pursue another dream – to become a trucker. He later established Doc Morgan Trucking and hired three more truckers. Often, when driving his 18-wheeler, to Morgan's great amusement, he sported a tan derby hat with a red feather.

When the practice sold, Cynthia joined the Indian Health Service in Santa Fe and Morgan began her freshman year at the University of New Mexico.

Morgan laughed out loud one time when she read a newspaper clipping her mother showed her, with a photo of Doc standing in front of his deep metallic blue Kenworth T600. When asked by the newspaper reporter what his wife thought of his selling a successful medical practice to become a trucker, he said, "I've been so busy doctoring and trucking I never got around to finding Mrs. Morgan." A second photo showed him winking. "One of these days I'll find her."

* * *

The familiar gray cinderblock building lay just ahead with two Doc Morgan Trucking rigs parked beside it. Vicky Lovato, Doc's secretary, greeted Morgan warmly when she entered the front office. Morgan smiled at the sound of Doc Morgan speaking with someone on the telephone in the next room. While she and Vicky visited and caught up on gossip, Doc emerged from his office with his customary grin and warm embrace.

"I'm on my way to Fort Collins, Doc." She raised her eyebrows in anticipation of a difficult goodbye.

"Thank you for coming by, Morgan." He waved his hand toward his office. "I know you need to be on the road, but have a seat so we can visit for a couple of minutes."

Morgan preceded Doc and sat in one of the two chrome and leather guest chairs in front of his desk. Doc sat in the other guest chair and turned it to face her. "I just want you to know, Morgan," he peered at her over the top of his rimless glasses, "how very proud I am of you. You graduated from UNM and are now on your way to one of the best vet schools in the country. That is quite an accomplishment." His grin returned. "And your mom named you Morgan. In addition to being proud, I am honored."

Morgan folded her hands on her lap while her mind raced to find the words to thank this giant of a man, this kind and generous human being who changed the lives of her mother and herself. "Doc, I stopped by to thank you for all you have done for mom and me." She glanced at the black and white photograph, behind his desk, of Cynthia and herself, taken when Morgan was four years old. They were astride her mother's favorite horse, Raven. "Without your moral support and the college fund you set up for me, none of this would be happening."

Doc nodded and smiled. "It gives me tremendous satisfaction to see you pursue your dream and… to be a part of it."

He raised his arm and swept it around the office and the trucking yard. "This is my dream. Doc Morgan Trucking. A successful medical practice provided the funds for me to become a trucker." He laughed. "Something I'd wanted to be since

I was a kid! And I own a trucking company to boot!"

He slapped his leg. "And now I get to participate in your dream, Morgan—your dream to become a veterinarian."

Her eyes moistened. "Thanks, Doc." She almost called him Dad.

He placed his hands on the arms of the chair and rose. Morgan stood and they hugged.

"Drive carefully."

Morgan felt her heart swell as she turned and left Doc's office. She must not disappoint this kind man.

Chapter 5

The day she arrived in Fort Collins to begin her first year of vet school, Morgan joined a tour of the CSU campus. Following the tour, she wrote to her mother,

This is a fantasy campus brought to life. It is beautiful. The grass, the trees, the landscaping, the buildings! I can't wait to walk with you and Nali around The Oval, one of the most lush spots I have ever seen. It is a campus landmark. More later.

Together, Morgan and Suki rented a small two-bedroom apartment near the Veterinary Teaching Hospital. At the end of the first week, Morgan woke from a deep sleep and glanced at the clock on her bedside table. Two A.M.

Suki sang in a soft voice as she opened the apartment door. "Come along and be my party doll, come along and be my party doll."

Until her freshman year in vet school, Morgan had paid little attention to song lyrics. By mid-October she knew the words to "Party Doll" by heart. At the sound of water running in the bathroom, she rolled over and went back to sleep.

One exception to Suki's partying was the spring semester of their first year when two very difficult classes, Veterinary Bacteriology and Veterinary Parasitology, kept both of them glued to their books.

Mother and Nalí, it seems all Suki and I do is memorize, and memorize, and memorize some more! There are so many long Latin names of teeny, weeny, tiny things in an animal's body. I am almost afraid to eat or touch ANYTHING, anymore!

A year later, she wrote:

Clinical Science is such a challenge. Suki and I do things with our minds and our hands while we learn. Sometimes it's confusing. One of my classmates is an older girl from Philadelphia. Her name is Brittany Jennison and she is 28 years old. Britt used to be a veterinary technician and she is good at explaining things. I really like her.

Both Morgan and Suki held their own academically. Financially, Suki's family was better able to provide for her than Morgan's mother and grandmother, but Morgan received welcome scholarship assistance from the Indian Health Service and the American Indian Graduate Center. And the college fund established for her by Doc Morgan helped tremendously.

Every Sunday they treated themselves to omelets at The Egg and I Restaurant, not far from the apartment and they frequently took hikes together on the mountain trails near Fort Collins. Around the CSU campus, they were known as the Kewa Sisters.

Morgan was grateful for Suki and Britt. With few Native Americans on campus, she sometimes felt like an outsider. With Suki or Britt, she was never alone.

Following one of their Sunday breakfasts, she telephoned her grandmother. "How are you feeling, Nalí?"

"As good as can be expected of an old woman in her eighties," Maria chuckled. "But slowing down. Your mother and I were talking about you and your friend, Suki, yesterday and the time you spent together at UNM. Are the two of you behaving yourselves?"

"Of course we are!" Morgan laughed. "Suki and me and our friend, Britt. I dearly love them both. We are like sisters."

"I would like to meet Britt. She sounds like a nice young lady. You still want to live in Shiprock someday?"

"Yes. I would like to know the Dinè. Your people."

"If the spirits wish it to happen, it will happen, child."

Morgan sensed her grandmother's voice becoming weaker. "I miss you, Nalí."

One night, after Morgan and Suki had finished their studies, they split a cold beer and spent several minutes gossiping and laughing before going to bed. Morgan put on her pajamas and sat on the edge of her bed. She reached across the small desk beside the bed and picked up a photograph of her parents on their wedding day.

In the photograph, her mother and father were seated at a dining table holding a wedding basket. The basket was filled with blue corn mush on which a medicine man had sprinkled corn pollen from east to west and south to north. Morgan's mother had told her all about it. After the bride and the groom had eaten the mush, their relatives joined them to feast on bread, mutton, tomatoes, and other tasty dishes. By tradition, many speeches followed the feast.

Her mother, now a widow, kept the basket in a special place—a small shelf in an arched recess in her bedroom wall.

Morgan never knew her tribal policeman father, killed three weeks prior to her birth. She was, however, extremely proud of

Jonathan Bluestone and their Navajo heritage. Whenever his name was spoken, it was done so with respect. In the photo he appeared to be a gentle man. She wished she had known him. She also wondered if her mother, Cynthia, would one day find another man.

She set the photo back on the desk and flipped the lamp switch. Then she pulled the black and white blanket woven by her grandmother snugly beneath her chin, and drifted off to sleep.

Chapter 6

Mid-May. Morgan and Suki and Britt had passed their junior year final exams and were celebrating over lunch in a corner booth at The Trail Head Tavern in the Old Town section of Fort Collins. Suki was seated between Morgan and Britt. Her straight black hair and brilliant blue eyes stood out against the burgundy colored booth.

She reached for their hands. "Hey guys, we knocked 'em down!"

"We had some close calls as you know," Morgan said. "Once or twice, I wondered if I'd pass. But thanks to Britt, I avoided going off the road too many times."

"We have to look out for each other, guys." Britt laughed.

Suki took a sip of beer and picked up her sandwich. "I'm proud of all of us."

Britt looked up from the napkin she had been folding and refolding. "Even though this process of becoming a vet is a long one and the pay might not be great, I'm grateful to have found a profession that I know I can look forward to each and every day."

"Not many people are as fortunate," Suki said,

"I realize we have another year to go—and it's going to be a challenging one—but I feel truly passionate about what we're doing. A friend back home is an opera apprentice and he loves the Italian composers: Verdi, Puccini, Leoncavallo. He's totally captivated by their works. I feel the same passion for the furry creatures placed in our care as he does for his music." Britt turned to Morgan. "Does that make sense?"

Morgan nodded. "Very much so."

"Heavy stuff, Britt. But right on." Suki raised her mug. "Here's to next year!"

Two days later, the three of them joined other members of their class at a Senior Orientation presentation and the beginning of the Senior Year Practicum. Their entire year would be devoted to clinical rotations.

Morgan and Suki sat on the grass in a tree-shaded area west of the vet hospital parking lot studying the information sheets and books they were given. Both were wearing jeans and green Colorado State University T-shirts.

"This is the real world, isn't it?" Morgan shoved her dark glasses up from her forehead to the top of her head.

"Where the rubber meets the road." Suki grinned her dimple grin. She glanced at one of the handouts: "It says here we can choose from thirty different hands-on clinical sessions during the year; both small animal and large animal."

"We're going to be busy, huh?"

"You bet we are, kiddo."

"I wish I had your self-confidence, Suki." She turned to her. "I really do. It would crush my mother and my nali if I failed."

Suki reached for Morgan's hand. "You are not going to fail, Morgan. You and I are both going to graduate." She lifted her eyes to Morgan's and tightened her grip. "That is all there is to it. Okay?"

Morgan forced a grin. "Okay."

* * *

Several months later, following an afternoon equine surgical procedure, Morgan returned to the apartment after dark and dragged herself up the stairs. After collapsing into bed she fell fast asleep.

A few hours later, she tossed and turned, then lay on her back staring at the white plaster ceiling, reviewing the surgery. Every few minutes, subdued reflections from passing headlights illuminated the room.

* * *

The surgery began at three o'clock. She and two of her classmates were scheduled to observe and assist the surgeon, an anesthesiologist, and one of the veteran nurses in a stand-up surgery in the neck and right shoulder area of a gentle chocolate brown mare.

The surgeon, Dr. Elizabeth Brown, a member of the faculty for twelve years, was married and the mother of two teenage sons. Morgan had witnessed two of her previous procedures and was in awe of her surgical skills

Dr. Brown involved Morgan in this surgery to an extent she had not expected. "I would not ask you to do this, Bluestone, if I didn't think you could handle it."

They both wore surgical masks, but could hear each other perfectly.

"Now, step forward and make the incision. I will be right here beside you."

* * *

As her eyes followed the headlight reflections across the ceiling, Morgan mentally repeated the surgical sequence from start to finish. She again experienced the same relief once the procedure concluded. Dr. Brown had even put her arm around her and congratulated her.

Yet… the mare was one of the most forgiving and beautiful animals she had ever known. There was something very special about the horse. She would never forget the trust in the animal's eyes when the surgery ended and she stroked her graying nose and muzzle. Perhaps that was what kept her awake. She had asked Dr. Brown if she could spend the night in the horse's recovery stall, but Dr. Brown shook her head. "The staff will care for her, Morgan. I promise."

Now after three hours without sleep, Morgan turned her head to the clock on the nightstand. 2:37 A.M. She rubbed her eyes, rolled over, and sat on the edge of the bed.

* * *

The mare was standing in her stall when Morgan opened the sliding door and stepped inside. She murmured a greeting nicker as Morgan took slow and gentle steps until she reached her side. Then she leaned her head toward Morgan as she scratched her left ear.

"How are you doing, girl?" Morgan said in a soft voice as she reached for her stethoscope. She placed the diaphragm against the mare's chest. Breathing was normal and the heartbeat was strong.

Morgan stood and rested her forehead against the mare's neck. "I'm so proud of you," she whispered. The shirttail from her cotton shirt hung outside her jeans and her hair needed combing.

Someone opening the metal door broke the silence in the stall. Morgan looked up.

"Need any help, Bluestone?" Barney Reid peered at her from beneath the brim of his cowboy hat.

Morgan shook her head and patted the mare. After a moment she turned and stared at Barney with tears in her eyes.

"Your first equine surgery?" he said.

She nodded. "I had to come check on her. To make sure I hadn't made a mistake."

Barney walked at a slow pace around the mare, patting her as he examined her. "She's going to be okay."

He paused for a moment on the opposite side of the mare. "She's going to be just fine." He continued around the front of the horse, rubbed her nose, then stood beside Morgan. "You are going to be one hell of a vet, young lady."

"What are you doing here? So late?"

"The front desk has standing orders to call me at home whenever a student comes in at night to check on an animal."

"Why?"

"They might need help." He patted the horse. "You never know." He scratched the gray stubble of beard on his chin. "And the desk told me it was you."

"Thanks." She looked down at her aged brown boots.

"How did you get here?"

"I walked. It's not that far."

"Let me drive you home in my pickup, Dr. Bluestone."

Morgan looked up. "Dr. Bluestone. I like the sound of that."

"Better get used to it." He placed his hand on her shoulder. "You'll be receiving your degree in a couple of months. It's not that far away!"

Morgan rubbed the mare's ear.

Barney reached back and opened the metal door to the stall. "Have you taken your national and state boards yet?"

"I'll take them next week."

"Worried?"

"Yes." She glanced back at the mare, standing in the middle of the stall with both eyes on her. The mare snorted. "I hope I'll do okay."

Barney's graying straight hair hung shaggy over his collar. He closed the metal door. "You'll do fine."

Morgan smiled. She liked Barney Reid. Doc Morgan would like him, too.

Chapter 7

Cynthia Bluestone flew from Albuquerque to Denver International Airport for the graduation ceremonies. Morgan met her at the airport in the F150 pickup and they drove to Fort Collins. Morgan's grandmother had hoped to attend, but two weeks before they were to leave Kewa Pueblo, Nali tripped in their vegetable garden and broke two ribs falling against a small metal culvert.

"I'm concerned about your grandmother," Cynthia said to Morgan while she unpacked her suitcase at the apartment.

"Is she still in the hospital?"

"She's back home now. A nurse friend of mine is checking on her while I'm gone." She sighed. "But age is taking its toll. I am afraid she's approaching the end of her journey."

"She is in my prayers."

"In mine as well."

Two days later, Morgan felt her grandmother's presence as she walked across the stage to accept her diploma—wearing Nali's silver and turquoise bracelet. She sensed her hand, beside hers, receiving the certificate.

That evening Doc Morgan telephoned from Albuquerque to congratulate *Doctor Bluestone!* "Young lady, I am very, very proud of you!"

"I can just picture you, Doc, seated at your desk, wearing

your tan derby with its red feather!" She laughed. "I couldn't have done this without you."

"The pleasure is mine, Morgan. Drop by when you get back and we'll share a cigar."

"I will, Doc!" She felt a tingling in her cheeks

"And give my best to your mother."

Her throat tightened. "I will . . ."

* * *

Suki Winters' mom and dad drove to Fort Collins from their ranch in Bozeman for the ceremonies.

Britt Jennison waited at the Denver airport for several hours for her parents to arrive from Philadelphia, but had to return to CSU without them. Their departure had been cancelled due to torrential rains in the region, so they caught a later flight. Her father, a Philadelphia trust attorney, broke speed records trying to arrive on time but they missed Britt's graduation by seventeen minutes. Seated beside Britt during the graduation ceremony, Morgan noticed her turning, every few minutes, surveying the audience for her parents. She reached for Britt's hand and squeezed it.

The day following graduation, Morgan, Suki, Britt, and their parents gathered at The Egg and I for a farewell breakfast. Their table was on the north side of the restaurant overlooking the parking lot. They had just placed their omelets order when Suki, seated next to the window, looked outside. "Hey, you guys, look at this."

Strutting across the parking lot from an adjacent park was a mother mallard with five ducklings lined up behind her, all waddling to a nearby pond.

Britt raised her coffee cup. "What a cool salute to three new vets! Those fuzzy little guys are beginning a new chapter in their lives. And so are we."

"I have one more stop to make before we leave here." Suki's blue eyes sparkled.

"Where's that?" Britt said.

"I need to say goodbye to Bart the Bear."

Morgan shook her head and smiled. "Bart is going to miss you and your visits before exams, Suki. Pat his paw and thank him for both of us."

* * *

Following breakfast, the three new veterinarians shared tears and hugs – and vows to stay in touch.

After Suki and her parents pulled out of the parking lot and Britt's family proceeded to the Denver airport, Morgan and her mother returned to the apartment to load a few remaining items into the pickup. As they prepared to leave, Morgan looked up at the apartment building and her old room on the second floor. "Lots of memories, Mom."

"I know," her mother said from the passenger side of the truck. Her white hair reflected the late morning sun; it was tied in a chongo, a Native American bun. She wore a dark blue velvet blouse and long black full skirt.

Morgan opened the truck door and eased onto the driver's seat. The bright green seat fabric was aged and torn after years of wear and exposure to high altitude sunlight.

"I'll never forget your first telephone call. You sounded so scared and homesick." Cynthia laughed. "But you worked things out pretty quickly."

"Thanks to you and Nalí." She turned the key in the ignition. "The two of you were always there."

Cynthia fastened the seatbelt and folded her hands on her lap. She turned to Morgan. "I am proud of you, Morgan. Our veterinary doctor."

"Thank you, Mom."

"I believe your father, my Jonathan, was with us at your graduation ceremony. I could feel his being with us." She smiled. "He is proud of you also. Very proud."

"I'm glad, Mom. I also felt Nali was there when I accepted my diploma."

Cynthia nodded. "I did as well."

"Mom," Morgan reached to her right to connect her seat belt, "Before we head home, I want you to meet my friend Shiwana."

"The buffalo calf?"

"Uh-huh. Only now he's a yearling. I am told that the herd may be transferred to a tribe or an open park sometime in the future."

They drove to the veterinary holding pens area and Morgan parked the pickup several yards from the gate. "Come on, Mom."

Cynthia stepped out of the truck and walked around beside Morgan. "You go and say goodbye to your Shiwana. I'll wait here."

Morgan walked to the wide metal gate and opened it. At the opposite end of the pen, the young buffalo came from beside his mother and watched Morgan as she closed the gate and stood inside the pen. He took a few steps toward her and stopped, raised his head into the slight breeze, then lowered it and continued walking. Morgan reached into her pocket and pulled out a sugar cube. She extended her hand and the yearling took the sugar.

"You take care of yourself, my friend." She leaned forward and scratched the top of his head. "I will always remember you."

The young buffalo snorted and rubbed his head against Morgan's leg.

As Morgan turned to leave, she caught her mother's eye and knew she had been watching her the whole time. When she nodded in understanding, Morgan felt at peace with the cloud spirits and with herself.

* * *

Three weeks later Maria Bluestone died at the age of 86. Despite the best efforts of her Albuquerque doctor and the Kewa Pueblo Medicine Man, her frail body gave out to an overpowering siege of pneumonia. Her passing strengthened Morgan's resolve to establish an animal clinic on the land of her grandmother, the land of the Diné.

Chapter 8

Garrison Greyeyes was in his senior year at Monument Valley High School, in the township of Kayenta, population five thousand. The township's northern boundary lay in the northeastern corner of Arizona, within eyesight of Utah and Monument Valley.

A well-built kid, Garrison played tight end on the Mustang football team. In the season just ended, the team won seven and lost four. He enjoyed sports, but, during this, his last year of high school, his mind was focused on graduation and what life held in store for him afterward. With persistence and luck, he hoped to find a job in a veterinary clinic.

The course he enjoyed most was the one for aspiring veterinary assistants. In the exam room during one of the mid-morning classes, Garrison held a medium-sized dark brown dog on the stainless-steel table while another student took the dog's vitals. The animal had been brought in by a neighboring sheep rancher who said it kept shaking its head and whining. The dog trembled, fearful of the strange people and unfamiliar sounds.

Across the table from Garrison was Dr. Frank Spruce, a visiting Native American veterinarian from Jemez Pueblo, New Mexico. Garrison guessed Spruce to be in his mid-thirties, young enough to relate to high school students and old enough to share wisdom and experiences of the real world of animal medicine.

"So what do you think is the ailment of our patient, Garrison?" Dr. Spruce said.

Garrison held the dog firmly but gently. "He must have an ear problem of some kind."

Spruce looked over the top edge of his glasses. "What makes you think that?"

"The way he keeps scratching and turning his head to the side."

"What else?" Spruce leaned closer to Garrison.

"When I touched his left ear, he whined."

The vet reached into a large pocket on his white smock and pulled out a zippered leather case. He unzipped the case and retrieved a black metal otoscope. "Let's take a look." He walked around the table and stood beside Garrison. "Turn the patient around so he is facing in the other direction."

Garrison did as he was told. He could feel the dog's heart beating. "It's okay, boy," he murmured.

Dr. Spruce leaned over, holding the otoscope in his left hand. He inserted the cone in the dog's ear and looked through the lens. "Someone hand me the three-and-a-half-inch alligator forceps."

One of the students picked up the forceps from several instruments lined up on a tray beside the table and placed it in Spruce's extended right hand. He inserted it into the dog's ear. The dog jerked and whined as the vet removed a foxtail grass seed covered with oily, yellowish wax. "This," he said, "is our patient's problem."

He handed the forceps and foxtail to one of the students. "Pass this around. Everyone look at it closely."

A female student, in her junior year, examined the foxtail

and wrinkled her nose. "Gross."

The vet glanced up at her. "Better get used to it if you're goin to work in an animal clinic."

She grinned with a sheepish grimace. "I know."

"Have any of you heard of *otitis*?"

Around the table, the students shook their heads.

"It is an infection of the ear canal. Look it up tonight and we'll discuss it tomorrow."

He glanced toward a stainless steel cabinet against a near wall. "Someone hand me that ear cleanser solution on the bottom shelf." He reached for the bottle. "And the box of cotton balls."

Another student handed him the box.

Garrison watched without blinking as Dr. Spruce carefully cleaned each of the dog's ears then massaged them. He let the dog shake his head after each ear was cleaned. Then he petted the dog. "Good boy. You're going to be just fine."

When the clinical class ended a few minutes later, Garrison Greyeyes carried the dog to the Small Animal Recovery Room and remained on the floor with him until he drank some water and curled up on a blanket in the corner of his cubicle.

* * *

The day following high school graduation ceremonies, Garrison sat at the kitchen table working on a bowl of corn flakes while his father read the weekly *Navajo Times*. His mother stood at the kitchen sink.

"Found a job yet?" his father said as he turned a page of the *Times*.

"Not yet. The only thing I saw was an opening at that convenience store downtown."

"Doing what?"

"Janitor work and stocking shelves. But I want to work for a veterinarian."

His father pushed the classified section of the newspaper across the table. Never known for lengthy conversation, he said, "Take a look at this." He tapped his forefinger above an ad which read:

New Veterinarian Office opening east of Shiprock in July. Need veterinary technician or office assistant. Telephone for appointment.

The ad gave a telephone number with a New Mexico area code.

"The job is in Shiprock, Dad. That's a long commute from Kayenta."

"Call 'em anyway," his father said. "Maybe they'll hire you and pay you enough so you can rent someplace."

"*If* they hire me. I'm not even close to being a veterinary technician. I'd need two more years of school. And I don't know anything about running an office."

"Call 'em anyway."

His mother turned around. "I don't want you to leave home."

"He's a big boy," his father snorted. "Time to let him go."

Garrison caught his mother's eye and said nothing. His father had spoken and that was the end of their conversation.

CLINIC

You don't enter this profession for money.
You enter it to help animals have a better life.
This is not a forty-hour-a-week job; it is a passion.

Stephen J. Withrow, DVM, DACVS, DACVIM
Director, Animal Cancer Center, Colorado State University

Chapter 9

Morgan admitted it wasn't much to look at, the single-wide mobile home on the outskirts of Shiprock, New Mexico. Used as an office for a used car lot until the business failed, the bank had repossessed the structure and small lot and was now eager to get the property off its books.

When Morgan and Cynthia expressed an interest in buying it and offered a reasonable down payment, the bank loaned them the balance, securing the loan with the building and the land. Doc Morgan's generous cash graduation gift made the down payment possible. The loan closing took place in Farmington. That night Morgan was so excited she could barely sleep.

The following day, she stood on her new parcel of land, on a bluff north of Highway 64. On the other side of the highway she counted scattered mobile homes; behind them, in a green fertile valley, farms along the San Juan River.

She turned around to face the building and folded her arms across her chest. With a major cleanup, some serious office remodeling, and a shingle on the door, the single-wide would soon become the clinic of Morgan Bluestone, Doctor of Veterinary Medicine. The parking area which had accommodated seven used cars and pickups with flashy signs and window paint would provide parking spaces for clients. The dirt road in front also offered plenty of room for a truck pulling a horse trailer.

* * *

"Mom, we have to get a picture of this." Morgan wiped her

forehead with her forearm, turning the sleeve of her denim shirt a dark blue. "Our *Before* and *After* pictures!" In one of her hands she held a sponge; in the other a towel.

"I agree." Cynthia grinned. "So we can look at them years from now and be totally amazed!" She stood at the bottom of the metal steps connecting the mobile home building to the parking area. "I wish your father and your grandmother were here to celebrate with us." She turned and walked to the pickup to retrieve her camera.

* * *

A short time later Morgan and her mother strolled around the structure with a local contractor from Farmington.

"The man at the bank told me this was originally a four-bedroom, two-bathroom mobile home with a living room and kitchen," Morgan said. "It was later converted to the used car office with adjoining rooms containing car parts, catalogs, and girlie magazines."

"I know," the contractor said. "I've driven past it a thousand times."

"Can you help us convert it to a veterinary clinic?"

"Let's go inside and look around," the stocky, heavyset man said. "You let me know what you want done and I'll give you an estimate."

They began in the rear inside area of the building.

"In this unused space," said Morgan, "I want to install a small bank of cages to house small animals being boarded or in recovery. On the west end of the building, we'll need added living quarters for future 24-hour staff, and I want a fenced enclosure behind the building to provide two corrals and a walking area for examining large animals."

Three weeks later, Morgan, her mother, and the contractor with his assistant had transformed the interior to a veterinary clinic with waiting area, exam room, operating room, recovery room, X-ray unit, secure medical vault, and small office for Morgan.

A day before the clinic grand opening, front page articles in the Shiprock and Farmington newspapers included news of Dr. Morgan Bluestone's new veterinary clinic on Shiprock's east side. Morgan picked up the Farmington newspaper she had left on a waiting area chair earlier in the day.

"They jumped the gun on us, Mom. We're not ready to open until tomorrow!"

"Don't worry. No one will show up today."

Next to the article in the Farmington newspaper was a photograph of Army Sergeant First Class George Lucas Begay, a wounded Navajo soldier, as he arrived at the Albuquerque International Airport. The accompanying article described his combat tour in Iraq. He was the son of Winston and Lorraine Begay of Shiprock.

"Do you know this Begay family, Mother?" Morgan said.

"There are many Begays in the Navajo Nation. I don't know them, but your grandmother may have been acquainted with them."

"He's a nice-looking man."

Cynthia looked over Morgan's shoulder at the newspaper photograph. "Yes, he is." She poked Morgan. "And probably married."

"*Mother!*" She continued reading the article. "And a brave warrior. He's headed for the VA Hospital in Albuquerque."

"And one of us is a veterinarian who is going to open her

office for business tomorrow!" Cynthia waved her hand. "Let's get to work."

"Will you help me inventory the medical supplies UPS delivered this morning?"

"I'll grab a pen and a tablet." Cynthia walked to the supply closet behind the receptionist's desk. "Have you finished interviewing for an assistant?"

"Only one interview to go." She ran her fingers through her hair as she looked down at the boxes of medical supplies stacked neatly on the floor. "A young man from the tech school over in Kayenta. Graduated this year. His family is from there, too."

Cynthia took a felt-tip pen from a box and placed it in her blouse pocket. Then she picked up a lined yellow tablet from one of the closet shelves. "When is he coming in for the interview?"

Morgan looked at her watch. "In fifteen minutes." She glanced toward the window facing the street. "My God, Mother!" She went to the window and separated the venetian blinds with her fingers. "Someone with a large horse trailer is pulling up outside!"

"Really! Your first patient? This is exciting!"

"But we're not open for business until tomorrow!" She looked around at the disorganized waiting area with boxes stacked on chairs. "Damn!"

They both stared out the window and watched an elderly white-haired cowboy step down from the pickup and walk across the parking lot to the front door. He sported a bushy handlebar moustache.

"Your first patient," Cynthia whispered.

"You've already said that. Why are you whispering, Mom?"

Just then the front door opened and the barrel-chested cowboy walked in. He turned to the two women looking out the window. "Do you ladies know where I can find the new animal doc?"

Morgan walked across the small waiting area. She held out her hand. "I'm Dr. Bluestone. How can I help you?"

The cowboy tipped his hat and held out his hand. It was rough and tanned and calloused. Morgan's hand was softer, but it was firm.

He removed the stained straw cowboy hat and glanced around the waiting area. "You open for business?"

"Not until tomorrow." She blushed. "But you are here now, aren't you?

The cowboy uttered a low soft chuckle. "Yes, ma'am. I guess I am. Someone told me you were already open. Said they read it in the paper."

"Well then, I guess we're open! And you are our first client." She turned. "This is my mother, Cynthia Bluestone."

Cynthia smiled and nodded. "How can we help you, Mister…?"

"Name's Lewis. Henry Lewis. I've got a ranch over near Farmington." He pushed the door closed behind him. "And I've got a sick horse out there in the trailer."

"What's his problem?" Morgan asked.

"It's a her. A mare. She won't eat. Just stands around doing nothing." He shook his head and stroked his moustache. "Lethargic. You know what I mean?"

"Let's walk over here to the reception counter, Mr. Lewis." As Morgan turned, the sound of tires spinning on gravel blasted through the open window.

Cynthia glanced outside as a beat-up Volkswagen bus skidded to a stop and a young woman stepped out with a Chihuahua in her arms. Cynthia headed to the door. "I'll take care of her."

Morgan had been holding the medical supplies invoice in her left hand for their inventory rundown. She folded it and shoved it in her back pocket and grabbed a clipboard with a tablet from a shelf beneath the counter. She set it on the counter top. "And how old is the mare, Mr. Lewis?"

"I'm looking for the new veterinarian!" the woman shouted. Her tan-colored Chihuahua barked.

Lewis scowled at the woman, then turned back to Morgan. "She is three years old,"

"Has she ever been bred?"

Cynthia attempted to take the young woman's arm. "Have a seat, please and Dr. Bluestone will be with you in just a moment."

"Who the hell are you?" The woman, who looked to be in her early thirties, jerked her arm loose. She sported bleached straw-blond hair and red painted fingernails.

Morgan's eyes widened as the woman took a step toward her. The chewing gum in her mouth smelled like stale bourbon.

"I had her bred a couple of months ago." Lewis glanced at the brazen blonde. "Wish that dame would shut up."

The Chihuahua bared its teeth at Lewis and growled.

"And?" Morgan said, turning her attention back to Lewis.

"And what?"

"Your mare was bred a couple of months ago."

"Oh, yes." Lewis frowned at the blonde. "A couple of months ago."

Cynthia spoke in a calm voice. "I am Dr. Bluestone's mother." She pointed to a chair in the waiting area. "Please have a seat and we will take care of you."

"I have two corrals out back." Morgan pointed over her shoulder with her pen. "Let me meet you back there and we'll guide the trailer in so I can take a look at her."

"My puppy has diarrhea." The woman's lipstick was thick and bright red. "She needs to see the doctor." She glanced down at the pink flowered towel beneath the dog. "Oh, God! She crapped again!"

Cynthia grabbed the roll of paper towels she had been using on the windows. She tore off several sheets and handed them to the woman.

At that moment, a young man opened the front door and walked in. He was a Native American in his late teens, well built, six feet tall with black hair and glasses. He wore khaki pants and a long-sleeved white shirt. He looked around at the chaos and grinned. "Showtime," he said in a soft voice.

Morgan wondered if the young man, who must have come for the scheduled interview, would turn around and escape the pandemonium. What he must think to see an older woman helping a blonde chick clean up Chihuahua poop, while at the reception desk, another woman talked to a cowboy who was getting upset at the noisy blonde. The phone rang and the Chihuahua raised its head and began to howl.

Cynthia rushed to the counter for the telephone and bumped into a potted plant the car dealer had left behind. The young man leapt forward and grabbed the plant before it hit the floor. The phone rang again and the Chihuahua howled louder. The man charged around the barrel-chested cowboy and took the phone from Cynthia's hand.

"Thank you." She looked up at him. "Are you here for the job interview?"

"Yes, ma'am."

She let out a grateful sigh. "Good."

"This is Dr. Bluestone's office. How can I help you?" He

pressed a hand against his other ear to block the racket.

"Will someone take care of my poor sick baby?" the Chihuahua woman cried while Morgan gave instructions to the cowboy to bring his trailer around to the rear of the building.

"Yes, we can help you with your goat," the young man said to the person on the phone. "Yes, Dr. Bluestone makes house calls. Would you like to make an appointment?"

Just then, another client walked in as Morgan turned to follow Henry Lewis outside. She observed the young man as he motioned the client to the reception counter.

Morgan stopped beside him. "Are you here for the interview?"

He cupped the phone. "Yes, ma'am."

"What's your name?"

"Garrison Greyeyes."

She held out her hand. "Garrison Greyeyes, you're hired!"

Chapter 10

Morgan hardly noticed as the days flew by with chaotic periods of highs and lows, triumphs and disappointments. Soon the small clinic's activities settled into more or less predictable routines. The staff of three—Morgan, her mother, and Garrison Greyeyes—managed to keep their ship on a steady course.

Morgan and Cynthia rented a small frame and stucco home not far from the clinic and, as part of Garrison's employment package, he was given the studio apartment on the west end of the clinic building. This greatly pleased his mother and father back home in Kayenta. The arrangement allowed him to stay within his budget and also to respond to emergencies and to monitor animal patients in different stages of recovery. A few emergencies he could handle by himself. Most, however, required a telephone call to Morgan and her making a quick visit to the clinic.

Cash income did not always keep pace with expenses and often, bartering of goods or services became, by necessity, the medium of exchange. Cynthia Bluestone had, through the years, accumulated savings, which she willingly shared with Morgan. Morgan made it a rule to never delay a payday for Garrison, since he did not have a financial cushion like the one provided her by Doc Morgan.

* * *

It was a mid-week morning. Early. The sun still rested beneath the eastern horizon, and to the west, the dark outline of the stone Ship Rock stood before the still darker sky.

Someone knocking on the front door of the clinic awakened Garrison. Not a hard knocking, but persistent.

He rolled out of bed and put on his jeans. Then he fished around with his bare feet for his slippers before walking down the short narrow hallway to the office area where the only light came from the outside porch light. He flipped the light switch for the office overhead lights and continued to the front door.

He opened the door and looked down. A young Navajo boy wearing tattered jeans and a white T-shirt held a black and white cat. "Can you help Tiger?" he said.

Garrison's gut tightened. "Please come in." He stepped back as the boy came inside. "What's your name?"

The boy held the cat close to his chest and looked around the waiting area. "Harold." He had neatly combed straight jet-black hair.

Garrison closed the door and dropped to one knee to be at eye level with the boy. "Harold, tell me about Tiger."

Harold's lower lip quivered. "She's sick. She won't eat." His eyes welled. "She throws up."

Garrison stood. "Let's walk over here to the examining room so I can take a look at her."

The boy clutched his cat and followed Garrison into the examining room. Tiger looked around the room with wide eyes. Her long tail dropped toward the floor.

Garrison turned on the ceiling light, then took the cat and placed it on a white towel spread on the stainless steel table.

"Help me lay Tiger on her side, Harold."

The cat offered no resistance. A healthier Tiger would have fought any attempts to lay her on the table.

Garrison ran his fingers gently across her abdominal area and stopped when he felt a bulge. "Harold?"

"Yes."

"I'm going to telephone Dr. Bluestone at home." He stroked the cat's head. "And ask her to come in and see Tiger. I'm not a doctor. Okay?"

"Okay."

* * *

Morgan wore a dark blue smock and had tied her shoulder-length brown hair behind her head with a simple copper barrette. She put on her glasses and began her examination of Tiger. Harold stood on the opposite side of the examination table, the top of his head barely above its surface.

Morgan placed her stethoscope against the cat's side. The cat's purr was irregular.

"Can you help Tiger?" Harold said.

"We are certainly going to try, Harold. What were her symptoms?"

"What do you mean?"

"What was Tiger doing before you brought her in?"

"Like I told him," he glanced up at Garrison, "she won't eat. And she throws up."

"Does she throw up blood?"

"Uh-huh."

Morgan listened to the cat's heartbeat and her strained breathing. She ran her fingers around the midsection and located the bulge Garrison had reported. A tumor. A very large tumor. Tiger's breathing became weaker and more shallow.

"Are your mother or father with you, Harold?"

He shook his head. "I walked down here by myself."

"But I have driven by your home and it's almost five miles from the clinic." She shook her head and gave him an admiring smile. "I have met your mother and father, Harold. They are both very nice. And Tiger is mighty lucky to have you."

His eyes widened. "Will Tiger be okay?"

"She has a tumor. Do you know what a tumor is?"

"It's big and bad."

"I'm afraid Tiger has one of those. I suspect a mast cell tumor."

She turned to Garrison. "Good preliminary diagnosis, Garrison. Thank you for calling me right away."

He nodded. "You're welcome."

"Can you fix it?" Harold pleaded.

She looked down at the cat. Her breathing became more labored. "I don't know, Harold."

She paused. "Tiger will require surgery. I will do my best."

Harold reached his fingers into the cat's thick fur. Morgan placed her hand on his head. "I need to talk to your mother or your father."

"Why?" His eyes began to water.

"Because you are not yet an adult and—"

"But Tiger might die."

"And it might be an expensive procedure, Harold." Morgan spoke in a low voice and rested her hand on his small shoulder.

"I have two goats and three chickens you can have, Dr. Bluestone. Please…"

"Harold, we can work something out. Give me your telephone number so I can visit with your father or mother."

He wrote the number on a prescription pad Morgan handed to him, then Garrison took his arm. "Let's go outside, Harold. I'll show you where we keep the horses and burros."

Within the hour, Morgan, with Cynthia assisting her, lowered the blade of a scalpel to make an incision in Tiger's abdomen while Harold and Garrison sat outside on the back steps leading to the holding pen.

Chapter 11

Tiger's mast cell tumor was removed and soon after her recovery, she returned home in the family pickup. The following Saturday, Harold rode his bicycle to Dr. Bluestone's clinic to begin a year-long job tending to the yard and the holding pens—in payment for Tiger's surgery.

* * *

The final client of the day, a Navajo elder, had just left with his sheep dog. Cynthia tidied up the exam room and put away instruments, then waved to Morgan before locking the front door and driving to the grocery store in Shiprock.

Garrison poked his head into Morgan's small office. "There are no boarders to care for this evening, Dr. Bluestone, so I'm going to go to my pad and fix something to eat."

Morgan glanced up from her desk. "You deserve a rest, Garrison. Thank you for your hard work today. I'll see you in the morning."

"Goodnight, Dr. B."

On the last day of the month, Morgan opened the center drawer where she kept the clinic checkbook and the bills. They were, for the most part, bills from vendors, utilities, and the bank's monthly loan payment, all of which she reviewed as they were received before placing them in the desk drawer.

The beat of rap music from Garrison's room drifted discretely down the hallway as she turned on the desk lamp and retrieved the checkbook. She reached for the bills and placed them between the lamp and the checkbook. The first check written was always to Garrison for his monthly salary; the second to the bank. The final check was to the animal feed store in Farmington.

She tabulated the deposits and withdrawals made during the month and froze in fear when she arrived at a balance of $24.73! She ran through the numbers one more time; then again. $24.73.

"Dear God in heaven!"

She placed her elbows on the desk and held her head. She had never expected to become wealthy from a veterinary clinic in the Four Corners area. But she hadn't realized she was walking this close to the edge. She bit her lower lip and became aware of the steady hum of traffic outside on the highway.

Many of her clients barely made ends meet themselves – but her acceptance of barter was perhaps more generous than it should be.

It was out of the question to apply to the bank for a line of credit. If the loan officer examined her present situation, he would shake his head and decline her request with a sincere apology.

Her mother had been generous already; she didn't want to ask her for more assistance.

Henry Lewis appeared to be a man of means, but it would be painfully embarrassing to ask him for a loan.

Suki and Britt were just getting started themselves, so she couldn't ask them for help.

Morgan folded her arms on the desk, lowered her head, and sighed. When the telephone rang, she jumped. "Hello."

"Morgan, it's ten o'clock. When are you coming home?"

"Ten o'clock?" She looked up at the brown circular clock on the wall above her desk. "Oh my God. I must have fallen asleep."

"Are you all right?"

"Yes, Mother. I'm okay." She reached for the checkbook and closed it.

"You've been working hard. Maybe you need to slow down."

"I'll be fine, Mom. I'll be home in a few minutes."

"I'm keeping your dinner warm."

Morgan picked up the envelopes to be mailed and withdrew the envelope containing a check for four hundred dollars to a medical supply company. She placed it in the checkbook and turned off the desk lamp.

Chapter 12

On Monday, the Tiger story repeated itself when Margaret Benally, a ten-year-old Navajo girl with long black hair and almond eyes held a puppy in her arms and stared up at Morgan. They were in the exam room. The child didn't say anything. Her words were in her eyes. *Please help my puppy.*

Her ten-week old puppy, very thin, came from the rez. He was a mixed-breed, light brown in color with floppy ears and shiny black nose.

Morgan took the dog from the girl's arms and placed him on the exam table. She put on her glasses. He had all the classic signs of distemper, including a nasal discharge and ocular discharge.

"What's your puppy's name, Margaret?"

"Buddy."

"Tell me about Buddy. Has he been sick?"

"Yes." The girl squinted at her, then down at the puppy.

"Throwing up?"

"Uh-huh."

"Pooping lots?"

"Uh-huh."

Morgan examined the dog. "He may have distemper."

"Can you get rid of it?"

"There is no cure yet for distemper, Margaret. But maybe

we can try to help Buddy to help himself. Leave him with me for a few days. We'll get some fluid into him and give him some medicine for his throwing up."

She placed the stethoscope diaphragm on the dog's chest. "Is that your mother out there?" She nodded toward a woman seated beside the door in the waiting area.

"Uh-huh."

"I'll need your mother's approval before I can proceed, Margaret. Do you think you could ask her to come in here so we can visit?"

"Okay."

Margaret's mother looked up at her and listened to her request to see the animal doctor. She rose and followed Margaret to the exam room. She wore a loose-fitting dark burgundy blouse and a long light-colored full skirt. Her shoes were canvas tennis shoes.

Morgan discussed her diagnosis with Mrs. Benally as well as the odds against Buddy's recovery. She then asked that Buddy be allowed to remain at the clinic to undergo close care. After a few moments, Mrs. Benally agreed to leave Buddy and Morgan motioned to Garrison to assist her with the pup.

Before she turned to check on the next patient, a middle-aged Navajo man knocked on the doorframe and motioned to his son to follow him into the exam room. She had met them at a feed store in Aztec recently when she and Garrison had bought animal feed and supplies. The man and his son ran a large flock of Churro sheep on the Reservation, west of Shiprock.

"Doc," the Navajo man said, "you gotta help us." He was of medium height with gray hair tied at the back of his neck in the traditional chongo. His skin was dark, weathered, and wrinkled. He took her arm. "We need your help."

Morgan glanced at the son, then the father. Her hands were in the large front pockets of her smock. "And how can I help you?"

"My father died." He glanced at his son, then back at Morgan. "Tom's grandfather."

"I'm sorry about your father and Tom's grandfather. And I apologize. I forgot your name."

"My name is Walter. Walter Yazzie." He seemed to gather his thoughts. "My father died last night. Our people... The Navajo... bury their dead quickly."

"I know. I am Dinè."

"My father and his horse have been together many years." He turned to his son, who nodded.

Tom sighed. "We will wrap my grandfather's body in a new blanket when we get back home and place it on his horse and we'll lead the horse to my grandfather's grave."

"Then," Walter continued, "his horse will carry my father on to his journey home."

"We need you to help us," Tom said.

"Will you help us? Will you euthanize my father's horse?" Walter asked.

Morgan slowly shook her head. "I'm sorry, Mr. Yazzie... and Tom. I cannot help you."

"Why not, Doc?" the elder said.

"Because I cannot euthanize a healthy animal."

"You told us you are Dinè."

"Yes. I am Dinè."

"Why will you not help my father's horse to accompany him into the spirit world?"

"Because, Mr. Yazzie, I do not have that authority. My personal beliefs, my values, my oath as a veterinarian do not allow me to take the life of your father's healthy horse."

"But—"

"Tom," she held up her hand, "and Mr. Yazzie. I am sorry. This is very difficult for me."

Walter Yazzie clasped Morgan's hand and held it with both of his. The room was silent.

"I understand." He nodded. "I understand." He took his son's arm and they walked out of the exam room.

Morgan removed her glasses, then reached for a tissue and cleaned them. She turned to search for Garrison and the puppy with distemper and found them in the small recovery room adjacent to the kennels. With Garrison's assistance, she gave the pup antibiotics to prevent his contracting pneumonia and began administering IV fluids to replace fluids lost to diarrhea and vomiting.

* * *

The following day's mail brought a check from an outfitter in Durango, in payment for a bill which was 60 days past due. Attached to the check was a letter of apology from the owner. Morgan breathed a sigh of relief and retrieved the envelope with her check to the medical supply company.

* * *

Three days later, Margaret Benally and her mother arrived at the clinic and asked to take Buddy home to continue his care themselves. Morgan hesitated before she consented. Several days passed and Mrs. Benally reappeared with Margaret standing behind her, carrying the pup.

"He was doing okay," Mrs. Benally said. "We thought he was getting well. Until yesterday when he started slobbering and falling down."

She looked at her daughter and the pup then back at Morgan. "Can you help?"

Facing the clinic's first euthanasia, Morgan's mouth became dry. She took the dog from Margaret's arms. "Margaret, I will try to help Buddy." She felt the dog's weak pulse. "Can you go out in the waiting area for a few minutes while I visit with your mother?"

Margaret nodded and left the room, closing the door behind her.

Morgan spread a towel on the exam table and gently laid the pup on the towel. Then she reached into a white wall cabinet and pulled a Euthanasia Consent Form from the lower shelf. "Mrs. Benally, I think we both know Buddy is dying."

The mother nodded. "Yes, I know."

"To save him further pain, I will need for you to sign this form authorizing me to put Buddy to sleep." She placed the form on the counter beneath the wall cabinet and handed Mrs. Benally a pen. The woman's hand trembled while she signed the form.

Morgan placed her arm around Mrs. Benally's waist and they walked to the waiting area where Margaret waited.

"Margaret, you take your mother back home and I will telephone her when I have something to report." She looked into the child's eyes. "Okay?"

Margaret reached for her mother's hand. "Okay." They walked out of the waiting area and through the front office door.

Morgan returned to the exam room and closed the door. She didn't stir until she heard a knock on the door.

"Need any help?" Cynthia said as she poked her head in.

"No, Mother, this is something I need to do by myself." She took a deep breath, then sedated the pup so she could administer the euthanasia. She injected the euthanasic agent, pink in color, into the vein of his left front leg. The next instant, Buddy exhaled and passed on peacefully. Morgan confirmed the heartbeat and the pulse had stopped.

She studied the lifeless animal on the table. "Mother, this is not what I went to vet school for… to put dogs down. We were taught to euthanize animals and it was difficult then." A faint rim of wetness appeared in her eyes. "But this is my first in my own practice."

"I understand." Cynthia took her hand. "But you will be called upon to do this again in your career, probably many times. And it will never get easier. You have cared for this animal and saved it from having to endure prolonged and excruciating pain." She squeezed Morgan's hand. "Garrison and I will take care of Buddy. You have more patients waiting to see you."

Morgan wiped her eyes then blew her nose. "First I must call Mrs. Benally and Margaret."

Chapter 13

Cynthia was seated at the receptionist's desk when the telephone rang. "Dr. Bluestone's clinic."

"This is the San Juan County Sheriff's Office. Is Dr. Bluestone in?"

"She is with a client and a patient at the moment. Can I help you?" She removed the yellow wooden pencil wedged above her ear and pulled a note pad across the desk.

"We have a deputy holding a guy north of Highway 64. Says he has been abusing his horse and needs a vet. Can you or the doc go out there?"

"Let me put you on hold for just a moment while I check with Dr. Bluestone."

"Okay, but hurry," he snapped.

Cynthia glanced in the examining room where Morgan had just finished removing stitches from a beagle's wounded leg. In the client waiting area, Bill Levy, a young local rancher wearing a John Deere baseball cap, waited with his black Labrador, Franklin. At two o'clock in the afternoon, no more appointments were scheduled.

She pressed the flashing button on the telephone. "Dr. Bluestone will be there. Give me directions."

Cynthia wrote the directions on a steno pad and placed it on Morgan's desk, then walked over to Bill Levy. "Dr. Bluestone has been called to an emergency out in the field, Mr. Levy. She'll give Franklin his rabies shot when she returns. And we won't charge you to leave the dog."

Levy grinned. "I like that." He scratched Franklin's ear. "Behave yourself, boy. I'll pick you up later." He stood and handed Cynthia the leash. "Will you telephone me?"

She patted his hand. "Of course I will."

* * *

To the west, near Shiprock, George Lucas Begay had just walked his fourteen-year-old daughter, Katie, to her yellow school bus and returned up the narrow road to his parents' home. A few months earlier, he had, received a medical discharge from the U.S. Army for combat wounds received in Iraq—the most recent from an IED, an Improvised Explosive Device.

The memories never left him.

* * *

Sergeant First Class Begay, commander of four security escort vehicles or 'gun trucks,' rode in the right seat of the lead vehicle near the town of Al Hasnimyah. He had just shoved the sliding window back and fired his M4 carbine at an ambushing gunman with an AK-47. A split second later came a violent wave of bright light, heat, and explosive thunder. The deafening blast lifted the vehicle several feet off the ground and threw it forward on its right side. The front tires were ripped to shreds and smoke poured out of the engine.

The blast threw George Begay's head against the door, slamming his brain against his skull, while sound and percussion waves shot through his body with devastating speed. The driver was lifted and thrown sideways on top of George, jamming him against the passenger door burrowed into the ground. The gunner, a farm boy from Boise, Idaho, died instantly.

Within minutes, George was airlifted by a Black Hawk helicopter to Balad Air Base Hospital, then by a C-130 Hercules to Ramstein Air Force Base, Germany. He had suffered traumatic brain injury, an injured sternum, three broken ribs, and damage to internal organs. Following surgeries and extensive therapy, he was transferred to Walter Reed Army Hospital in Washington, D.C. At Walter Reed, the supervising physician ordered a medical discharge for George with one hundred percent disability. George resisted the discharge but ultimately realized he must accept the decision and return to civilian life. He loved the Army and had worn the uniform proudly for 15 years.

A year prior to his deployment to Iraq, his wife, Mary was killed in an automobile accident between Shiprock and Farmington. George then sold the home he and Mary had owned and he and Katie moved in with his parents, Winston and Lorraine Begay. It was the same home he had lived in during his years at Shiprock High School. He was grateful to his parents for caring for Katie while he was overseas—particularly his mother for providing maternal guidance for her granddaughter.

* * *

Walking toward the house, George shivered at the approach of winter. Clear skies and cold blasts of northern air were replacing the giant thunderhead clouds of summer. The cold air aggravated the spinal injury caused by the IED. He shuffled into the house and found the back brace, a custom-fit gift from the

Veterans Administration Hospital in Albuquerque. He wrapped the brace around his torso and pulled the side straps forward and tightened them. Then he shoved his shirttail inside his jeans and walked outside to the corral.

He bridled the pinto, then threw on the saddle blanket and saddle. As he squatted beside the horse and reached beneath his belly for the cinch strap on the other side, he noticed a swollen area about six inches wide behind the horse's right front leg. He stood and stepped back for a moment, then removed the saddle and saddle blanket and examined the swelling more closely.

The pinto didn't move when he touched it, so there was likely little pain. He patted the horse. "Think I'll have a vet look at this."

The horse snorted.

He had heard of the new veterinarian and her clinic off the highway to Farmington and Bloomfield. Since he didn't own a horse trailer and wasn't even certain the pinto would ride in one, he decided to drive over to ask if she'd make a house call.

* * *

At the animal clinic, Morgan stood next to her mother while she read the note with directions from the San Juan County Sheriff. "Where's Garrison? I want him to hook up the horse trailer to the pickup."

"He's in the pen with the sorrel you treated this morning," Cynthia said. "He's been out there almost an hour."

"Is there a problem with the colt?"

"I checked on them a few minutes ago. The boy just loves animals."

"I want him to come with me. Can you take care of the

clinic if we both leave, Mom?"

"Of course, I can. I have been well trained!"

* * *

With her black medical bag in hand, Morgan, along with Garrison, stepped out of the truck and strode to the horse held by a halter and rope by the Animal Control Officer. The San Juan County Deputy Sheriff stood beside the patrol car. In the back seat, a wannabe cowboy from a northeastern city sat in handcuffs. Morgan learned he had tried to discipline the young horse with a rope of barbed wire until a neighbor drove by, witnessed the cruelty, and reported him.

"How can people do these things?" Morgan sighed as she did a quick examination of the horse's injuries before cleaning and disinfecting the wounds. After several minutes, she and Garrison were able to stop the bleeding.

The length of rusted barbed wire the Animal Control Officer had cut from the horse's neck was kept for evidence and placed in the trunk of the Sheriff Deputy's car.

"I think you're going to be okay, girl." She patted the horse's nose and heard a low, contented blow. "I'm going to ask Garrison to load you on that horse trailer hitched to our pickup."

She nodded to Garrison, who stood on the other side of the horse rubbing her shoulder with gentle strokes. "Then we'll take you to our clinic."

Garrison checked the halter and rope, and then led the horse to the trailer.

"You want to file charges, Doc?" The Deputy Sheriff's hands were on his hips.

Morgan stared at the pale specimen of manhood in the back

seat. "Yep. Extreme animal cruelty."

The wannabe turned to the open window. "My dad's a lawyer in New York," he hissed. "Don't mess with me, lady."

The Deputy Sheriff cleared his throat. "What do you think, Doc?"

She spat in the dust beside the wannabe's door. "File the charges."

"I'll so advise the County Judge." The Deputy grinned. "I like your style."

Morgan turned east toward the sound of an approaching pickup, bumping down the rutted road in a cloud of dust.

"That'd be George Begay," the Deputy said.

George arrived in a spray of powdered sand and dirt and stopped beside the patrol car. He turned off the engine, opened the truck door, and stepped down, still wearing his cowboy hat. In the passenger seat of the pickup Morgan saw a medium-sized sheep dog. The dog jumped out and followed closely behind him.

The Deputy held out his hand. "Hi, George." The Animal Control Officer nodded to George.

George shook hands with both men. Then he turned to Morgan and tipped his hat. "You the new vet?"

"Not quite new." She nodded. "I've been here awhile."

"Your assistant at the clinic told me I'd find you out here."

"The assistant you spoke with is my mother." She rolled her tongue against the inside of her cheek.

A light northern wind blew across the dry sparse grassland. To the north were the purple-gray mountains of southern Colorado.

"I see the resemblance." George chuckled. "And then some."

Morgan shoved her glasses to the top of her head. Sweat

beaded on her forehead and the mare's blood smeared the front of her blue denim work shirt. She slipped her hands into the back pockets of her jeans. "How can I help you?"

"I need you to take a look at my horse. He has a swollen area behind his front leg."

"I'll take a look at him after Garrison and I get this horse back to the clinic." She squinted in the bright sun, then raised an elbow to shield her eyes. "And you are George Lucas Begay."

"Yep." He raised his head. "How did you know?"

She grinned. "I've heard about you."

"Are you Dinè?"

"I grew up in Kewa Pueblo."

"Used to be Santo Domingo?"

"The tribe has always been Kewa. The Spaniards arrived with their soldiers and priests on a Sunday and changed the name to Santo Domingo."

"Holy Sunday."

"Now the pueblo is back to its original name, the way it belongs." She reached down and pet George's dog. "My grandmother was Dinè. She died recently."

"I'm sorry."

"She's with the spirits now."

The Deputy Sheriff and Animal Control Officer had been standing to the side.

"We'll take the suspect into the jail, Doc," the Deputy said. "Will you need any help loading the injured horse?"

"Thanks for offering, but you have work to do." She turned to George and winked. "Mr. Begay might be available to help Garrison and me if we need it."

George straightened his back and winced. He glanced at Morgan and cracked a grin. "I can probably manage that."

Morgan saw the outline of George's back brace beneath his shirt. The wind blew a strand of her dark brown hair across her forehead. She studied his face. A warrior's face. And he was more handsome than the newspaper photograph.

* * *

As they walked to the patrol car, the Animal Control Officer said to the Deputy. "She's a good-looking woman."

"Yeah, she is," the Deputy said.

"Is she married?"

"I don't think she is."

"You're not married. Ask her out."

The Deputy grinned. "You think so?"

Chapter 14

The clock on Cynthia's nightstand read 6:07 AM when she reached for the telephone. The light was on in the bathroom between their bedrooms while Morgan took a shower.

"Yes?" she said.

"Cynthia?"

"Yes, it is. Is this Vicky?"

"Doctor Morgan died last night."

Vicky, Doc's office manager. Cynthia rolled over and reached for the nightstand light. "Oh my God, Vicky. What happened?"

"Day before yesterday he got tangled up with a tie rope on one of the flatbeds and hit his head on the loading platform. They took him to Presbyterian Hospital here in Albuquerque. He died last night."

Cynthia leaned forward and held her head. Her arm rested on her knee. "Vicky, I am *so* sorry."

"You're the first one I called. You were his office nurse for lots of years. Doc really liked you."

She rubbed her eyes. "What a dear, dear man. Morgan will be devastated. He was almost a father to her."

"I know. He was like a father to me, too." Vicky paused. "Sally Tremaine, his lead driver and a very close friend, will take over the trucking company."

"Will there be a service?"

"You know Doc…" Vicky sighed. "He left instructions. No obituary, no funeral, no nothing."

"Sounds like Doc."

Morgan had finished her shower and stood in a white ter-rycloth bathrobe at the foot of Cynthia's bed.

"But, Cynthia…" Vicky said.

"Yes."

"Sally Tremaine and I are having a memorial anyway. We talked a few minutes ago." Vicky paused. "It will be here at the company office."

"Morgan and I will be there."

Cynthia ended the conversation and put the phone down. She stood and took Morgan in her arms. "Doc Morgan died last night."

Morgan rested her head against her mother's shoulder. "I can't believe he's gone." Tears filled her eyes. "He was such a kind man. Such a good man."

Cynthia looked at Morgan through her own tears. "He cared for both of us. Very deeply."

* * *

Doc Morgan had requested cremation, with his ashes scattered somewhere near Sandia Mountain, east of Albuquerque. Ten days after he died, a convoy of close friends and trucker buddies carried out his wishes from a high overlook near the top of the mountain. Everyone then gathered for a catered dinner at the cinder block office building of Doc Morgan Trucking.

The four Doc Morgan Trucking rigs were parked facing the building. Doc's Kenworth was on the left; beside it, Hoot 'N' Holler's robin-egg-blue Kenworth; then driver Slim Perkins' dark green Peterbilt. The fourth rig, on the right, was Bob Harper's root beer brown Freightliner.

Among those attending were Cynthia and Morgan. The black-and-white photograph, taken of the two of them astride Raven when Cynthia was Doc's office nurse, still sat on his desk.

Sally Tremaine and Dixie O'Donnell, two of the original truckers with Doc Morgan Trucking, introduced themselves to Cynthia and Morgan. Sally and Dixie were known on the road and in the trucking community by their handle, *Hoot 'N' Holler*. With them was Sally's husband, Bob Harper.

"We were both devoted to Doctor Morgan." Cynthia held Sally's hand and told them of Morgan's newly established veterinary clinic in the Four Corners area.

Morgan looked at the photograph. "After my father died, Doc Morgan made it possible for me to go to college and to become a veterinarian."

"He spoke often of both of you," Sally said. "With genuine affection."

The women visited, then Cynthia and Morgan said their good-byes and edged toward the office exit to return to Shiprock. They stopped in front of a color photograph of Doc Morgan which Vicky had placed near the office entryway. Cynthia wiped her eyes with the paper napkin she had been holding, then she and Morgan walked in silence to their pickup.

Morgan's mind and body were running on empty. The immense gratitude and love she felt for this kind man were all that had kept her moving forward. She opened the passenger side door for her mother, then closed it and walked around the back of the truck to the driver's side. She rested her hand on the door handle and gazed upward at the turquoise blue sky then to the Jemez mountain range. Above the mountain range, glorious thunderhead clouds. The cloud spirits.

She felt Doc Morgan's presence and she heard his voice. "Thank you, Doc," she said.

Chapter 15

George Begay woke up as he always did, when it was dark outside and no one else yet stirred. He visualized Katie sound asleep in her bedroom next to his, and down the hall beside the living room, his mother and father sleeping in their room.

Through the open window, he heard an 18-wheeler heading south on Highway 491, Reminded him of the 18-wheelers and gun-trucks speeding down Main Supply Route Tampa in central Iraq.

And the IED blowing up, ending his Army career.

His mind drifted to Morgan Bluestone, the attractive veterinarian. He'd thought about her a lot. Was there someone else in her life? Was it just she and her mother? Would Katie like her? Would she like Katie?

In the distance a pack of coyotes howled. He stood and stretched, knowing outside in the corral, his pinto and the sheep and chickens watched the back door listening for his whistle and his morning greeting. He got dressed. The day had begun.

Two hours later, he and Katie were seated at the breakfast table with his parents. "Katie," he said, "I have errands to run in Shiprock. I can take you and Anita to school if you want, so you don't have to ride the bus."

"Ooooh, neat! Anita will like that. I'll run next door right now and tell her."

"Say hi to her mama and her grandma for me, and let them know I'll call them later," said Lorraine, George's mother.

"You two girls!" Katie's grandfather Winston chuckled as he shook his head. "You look so much alike, people think you're sisters."

"That'd be okay with me!" said Katie with a grin.

* * *

Later, George and the girls waited at the school bus pick-up point. The Ship Rock stood majestically southwest of town, bathed in early morning sunlight. George waved the driver on and he tooted the horn and tipped his baseball cap. George's dog, Airborne, named for his years as an Army paratrooper, sat on the bench behind the front seat. Beside Airborne was a wooden fruit crate with a Plymouth Rock hen.

Katie looked over her shoulder. "Where are you going with Lois, Dad?"

George smiled. "I'm taking her by the new veterinarian's office."

"Why?"

"Lois has quit laying eggs."

Anita wrinkled her nose. "Do you guys name your chickens?"

"Only Lois," George said. "My mother named her. She has more personality than the other chickens."

"I think you just want to see the lady veterinarian," Katie said.

"She sure took good care of my horse."

"My dad says she's a good-looker, Mr. Begay." Anita joined Katie with a giggle.

"Come on, you guys. Lois isn't laying eggs and I think Dr. Bluestone can help her."

From the back seat came a *cluck, cluck, cluck.* They all erupted in laughter.

George slowed down. "There's your school, kids."

Cluck, cluck, cluck.

* * *

George set the crate on the receptionist's counter in Dr. Morgan Bluestone's Veterinary Clinic. No one else waited in the client area. Lois's head darted from side to side in response to the strange noises and voices. She pecked at George's fingers if they got too close to spaces between the wooden slats.

"Mr. Begay." Cynthia rose from the receptionist's desk. "We met several weeks ago when you came in about your injured pinto."

"Yes, ma'am. That horse is fine now. Dr. Bluestone knows her stuff."

"How can we help you today?"

George smiled from beneath the brim of his carefully formed straw cowboy hat. "Is Dr. Bluestone in?"

"She's in surgery at the moment. Perhaps I can help you."

George flashed an impish grin. "My chicken quit layin' eggs."

Cluck, cluck, cluck. Lois scratched the bottom of the wooden crate.

"I see." Cynthia looked at Lois in the crate. Lois returned the look and resumed scratching. "We haven't yet had the opportunity to work with chickens."

"I understand." He chuckled. "Her name is Lois."

"Excuse me?"

"The chicken. Her name is Lois."

Cynthia leaned forward. "Hi, Lois." She laughed and brushed her hair back. "God, here I am talking to a chicken!"

"I do it all the time."

"Dr. Bluestone's surgical procedure will require another hour or so. Perhaps we could make an appointment."

"Do you think she would like to go to the Gathering of Nations Powwow in Albuquerque on Saturday?"

"Aha!" She laughed. "Men!"

"What's wrong?"

"I think that's why you and Lois are paying us a visit this morning." She winked. "The Gathering of Nations is a very big event, isn't it?"

"About seven hundred tribes. You want to come?"

Cynthia laughed. "As the chaperone?"

"I can bring my daughter, Katie, too. And her friend Anita Tsosie."

"Mr. Begay, that sounds like fun!"

"Call me George."

"George," she pointed at the hen, "you bringing Lois?"

* * *

Morgan read the opening information about the arena.

"The University of New Mexico University Arena in Albuquerque is also known as 'The Pit.' It seats more than 15,000 and serves primarily as the home court of the University of New Mexico basketball team. It is also used for special events such as The Gathering of Nations. From around the world, primarily from the North American continent, indigenous tribes gather each year in a renaissance of cultural traditions to celebrate and to compete. Competitions range from dances to singing to drummers and the crowning of Miss Indian World."

George, Katie, and Anita Tsosie were seated closest to an aisle in the huge arena and Morgan and her mother were seated to their right. Morgan gasped as hundreds of dancers entered the arena down the steps from all four sides. Her spine tingled at the color, the pageantry, ornate headdresses, deep thundering drums, dancers spinning, and feathers flying. Everyone in the vast arena, it seemed to Morgan, shared a sense of identity with those around them— indigenous peoples coming together as one.

Morgan sat forward during the final competition for Miss Indian World, since she had read about it as one of the most prestigious and awaited events at each year's Gathering of Nations. Each contestant was tested in her public speaking, her knowledge of her tribe and its history, as well as her dancing and her personality.

Katie and Anita chattered about the beauty of the winner, Teyotsihstokwathe Dakota Brant, a member of the Mohawk Turtle Clan from Six Nations of the Grand River Territory, Canada. She had entered the arena a few minutes after one of the dance competitions ended, and several people gathered around her. She smiled and shook hands with everyone.

The two girls stared as George and Morgan watched them. "You two girls want to go down there and meet Miss Indian World?" George said.

"I'd be afraid to," Katie said.

"Me, too," Anita said.

"What if all of us go down?"

"*Really?*" Katie squealed.

"Really!" He stood. "Come on!"

"The four of you go down," Cynthia said. "I'll stay here and keep our seats."

George winked at Cynthia, then led the way while Katie and Anita followed between him and Morgan. They joined the circle of admirers just as a photographer from The Navajo Times snapped a few pictures.

He motioned to George. "Sir, will you and your wife bring your daughters over here so I can get a shot of you with Miss Indian World?"

Morgan waited in silence as George glanced at the eager faces of the girls. "Uh, sure… of course." He stood beside Morgan and the photographer positioned the two girls in front of them.

Dakota Brant reached out for Katie's and Anita's hands and asked them questions while the photographer's camera flashed and whirred. She then turned to George and Morgan. "Your daughters are beautiful."

Morgan blushed, "Thank you."

Other admirers charged forward to meet the charming Miss Indian World and to shake her hand, and the four of them slipped away.

They returned to their seats and a beaming Cynthia. "You girls looked like you were having fun! Tell me what happened."

George chuckled. "I bet each of them is promising herself that one day she will wear the crown."

The comment was ignored as the floodgates of animated reporting opened when Katie and Anita became a chorus of two, each eager to share her moment with royalty!

George excused himself to purchase souvenir programs

for everyone. When he returned a few minutes later, Morgan glanced at him. His blissful expression hadn't changed. She wondered if he were snapping mental pictures of all of them seated together with the girls talking a mile a minute. After a while, Morgan observed Cynthia's arm extended behind Anita with her hand resting on Katie's shoulder. Anita stopped talking to examine the exquisite silver and turquoise necklace resting against Cynthia's dark velvet blouse.

Cynthia glanced at George. "We thought you were lost."

Morgan placed her hand on George's arm. "Thank you for doing this."

"You're welcome." His brown eyes brightened. "Can't wait to see if our picture appears in *The Navajo Times*."

"With our daughters!"

The next weekly issue of the *Times* carried a front-page photograph of Miss Indian World, greeted by George Begay and Dr. Morgan Bluestone of Shiprock with Mr. Begay's daughter, Katie, and her friend, Anita Tsosie. The newspaper had done its homework.

Chapter 16

After working together for nearly a year, Morgan, Cynthia, and Garrison had all become effective multi-taskers.

"We can almost read one another's minds and, on occasion, can communicate without saying a word," Morgan commented one morning prior to opening. "I am so proud of our young clinic."

Mondays were always busy, particularly in the morning, with most clients needing care for their domestic pets—dogs and cats. In the Four Corners ranching area, house calls sometimes also became necessary. The Monday morning following the Gathering of Nations was no exception.

The telephone rang while Cynthia helped a customer complete some paperwork. She reached across her desk and picked up the cordless phone.

"Dr. Bluestone's clinic."

"Is this Cynthia Bluestone?"

"Yes, it is.

"Listen. This is Henry Lewis. Is Dr. Bluestone in?"

"She just wrapped up a consultation with another client, Mr. Lewis." Cynthia saw Morgan leaving the exam room and walking toward the receptionist's desk. "I'll hand her the phone."

Morgan took the phone from her mother. "Hello."

"Henry Lewis here, Doc."

"Henry!" Morgan smiled. "It is good to hear your voice."

"Thanks, Doc. Me, too. I may be needing your help."

Morgan pictured the big white-haired cowboy with his bushy handlebar moustache. "Go ahead."

"Remember the mare you helped me with a while back? Rusty? She had the intestinal problem?"

"Sure do."

"Well, she was pregnant just like we thought."

"Is there a problem?" Morgan walked behind Cynthia's desk and faced the National Geographic poster of a Yellowstone buffalo herd hanging on the wall.

"No, not yet. But," Lewis paused, "she is my prized mare and, as you know, this is her first foal. Her eleven-month gestation period has been pretty much normal. I think she's getting close. That's why I'm calling."

"Give me the signs." Morgan wore the dark blue smock. Her stethoscope was coiled in one of the large pockets.

"She started waxing—that tan waxy substance on the ends of her teats."

"Okay. What else?" She looked down, mentally picturing Rusty's condition.

"My foaling experience tells me she's a day or two away from delivery."

"That is correct, Henry. Where is Rusty now? Out in the pasture or in the barn?"

"Just before I called you, the ranch foreman moved her into the barn into one of my large stalls."

"What bedding do you have in the stall?"

"I had the boys put straw in there. Not shavings, if that's what you're wondering."

"You're doing all the right things."

"Will you be around in case I need you? My place is ten, fifteen minutes, from your clinic."

"Yes, I remember. I'll be here, but let's not wait until there's a problem. Call me as soon as you or your foreman sees Rusty's first stage labor."

"Okay, Doc." His voice sounded tense.

"You've obviously been through this before, many times. When she gets nervous and walks around in circles, getting up and down. You know the signs."

"Yeah, I know the signs. But Rusty is special."

"Don't worry, Henry. You and I will work together."

"Thanks, Doc."

"There might be some vaginal discharge. I want you or your foreman to give me a heads-up when you see some of these things. Call me. If I'm with another patient, explain the situation to my mother or my assistant, Garrison."

Henry took a deep breath. "I'll call you."

"And Henry…"

"Yes, ma'am."

"Unless there is a problem, a mare likes to be left on her own, without human interference."

"Yeah, I hear you."

Morgan had total confidence in Henry Lewis and his judgment. She put the phone down and moved on to the next patient.

* * *

The following morning, Garrison Greyeyes leaned across his bed and turned off the raucous thrift store alarm clock. He groaned and rolled over. Then he sat on the edge of the bed and scratched his head. The clock's face showed 6:00 AM. He yawned again and turned on the bedside light.

"Showtime," he mumbled as he plodded to the small bathroom a few feet away.

He showered, dressed, and prepared the morning coffee in the small kitchenette, then he began the morning routine of turning on lights and checking the animals in the recovery and boarding areas. This morning, only two small dogs and a cat. He finished ministering to the animals when the telephone rang.

He patted one of the dogs, closed her metal-framed gate, and walked to Cynthia's desk. "Dr. Bluestone's Animal Clinic."

"Is this Garrison?"

"Yes sir."

"Garrison, this is Henry Lewis. Dr. Bluestone asked me to call her when my mare got to first stage labor."

"Dr. Bluestone told me to expect your call, Mr. Lewis."

"Well, she's in first stage labor and I know it's early in the morning. Do you know how to get ahold of Dr. Bluestone?"

Garrison nudged his glasses up the ridge of his nose with his forefinger. "I'll call her at home." He glanced up at the round white wall clock. 6:45 AM. "She may decide to go directly to your ranch. I can take care of things here at the clinic."

"Thanks, son. Can you phone her right away?"

"As soon as we hang up, Mr. Lewis."

* * *

Twenty-five minutes later, Morgan arrived at the Lewis ranch in her pickup and ran to the barn with her black nylon MedPac containing instruments, medications, and supplies. Henry Lewis and his ranch foreman, Terrell Lee, a Navajo cowboy in his mid-thirties, stood outside the stall, out of the mare's sight. Morgan joined them at the wide observation window.

Rusty's water bag had just ruptured and second stage labor begun. She lay on her side. Right away, Morgan knew that the foal was beginning to enter the birth canal.

The mare strained to push the foal out. The foal, in a diving position, was emerging with the tips of its front hooves visible. Soon its nose and head edged forward resting between its forelegs. The mare pushed again.

Henry Lewis and Terrill Lee stood nervously on either side of Morgan. Henry lifted his cowboy hat and wiped his forehead with his arm. The mare pushed once more and the body of the foal emerged, then its hind legs.

Rusty remained on her side for a few minutes. When the foal struggled and Rusty stood, the umbilical cord broke.

Morgan quietly entered the stall. She approached the foal and removed the placental membrane from its face and wiped the fluid from its nostrils. Henry Lewis waited behind her, while Terrill Lee stood behind Lewis.

The three anxious observers stepped back and allowed the mare and her foal to proceed at their own speed. All three resisted any further urges to assist.

Thirty minutes later, the unsteady foal staggered to his feet. When the placenta passed, Terrill Lee saved it for examination by Dr. Bluestone.

Soon the colt searched for breakfast. When he found his mother's teats, he took hold of one and sucked, enjoying his first meal.

A couple of hours later, as Henry stood by her side, Morgan stroked the dark brown colt. "There is nothing more beautiful than a newborn foal." She then reached out and scratched

Rusty's ears. "Good work, girl." She rested her forehead against the mare's neck.

"Doc, you're an amazing lady." Henry spoke a little louder than a whisper. "You don't know how much I appreciate your being here. I was really worried about Rusty."

"I know you were, Henry." She patted the mare. "But she's going to be okay. She'll be just fine." She glanced down at the foal. "So will the colt. This was a textbook delivery."

"You'll send me a bill, won't you?"

"Yes, I will. And if there are any problems or complications, contact me right away."

Terrill Lee, standing beside Henry, held out his hand. "Thanks, Doc."

Morgan shook his hand and smiled. "You're welcome, Terrill." She picked up her medical bag and walked through the immaculate barn to her pickup.

* * *

After Morgan left, Henry and Terrill walked out of Rusty's stall and closed the gate.

"She's a nice lady, Mr. Lewis."

"Indeed she is, Terrill. And a damned good vet."

"Single?"

Henry turned and grinned. "Uh-huh."

* * *

As she lifted her MedPac into the pickup, Morgan thought of George. Where was he and what was he doing?

Chapter 17

When Morgan returned at mid-morning from Henry Lewis's, she once again appreciated how the clinic had become a seasoned animal hospital with its own antiseptic and animal smells, sounds of feathered and furry creatures, and high energy level.

The place was busy. Cynthia and Garrison conferred with clients or treated animal patients while other clients waited with animals in the lobby.

On her desk were several telephone messages. The first was written by Cynthia: "George Begay called. He wants to take you to a movie in Farmington."

On another message, in Garrison's handwriting, was the telephone number of Dr. Britt Jennison in Philadelphia. "Call her right away."

Morgan visited briefly with Cynthia and Garrison, saw that everything was under control, and returned to her small office to telephone Britt.

Following their pleasantries and chit-chat, Britt said, "You won't believe what I read in today's Inquirer. A wildlife park in central Pennsylvania just received a small herd of bison from northern Colorado!"

"Wow, Britt, I hope they enjoy the lower altitude and the lush green grass in front of Independence Hall!"

"Independence Hall is here in Philly, girl! Not in central

Pennsylvania!"

"I know." Morgan laughed. "How many head are in the herd?"

"A dozen or so I think. And there's a young bull, Morgan, five or six years old. A beautiful animal. With a white spot beneath its left eye."

"No kidding!"

"I'm going to drive over there one day soon, if I can get away from the office, to check them out. I'll take a picture of the young fellow and send it to you. It might well be the calf you knew when we were in vet school."

"Would you really? I adored that little guy."

"I know you did."

"I named him Shiwana."

"I remember when you did that, but forget what it means."

"Shiwana are the cloud spirits who live in the sky. Very often they protect us. I chose that name because the white patch looks like a tiny cloud."

"I love it… Shiwana."

"Britt, I remember reading of a terrible flood in Pennsylvania several months ago where two bison died. One of them apparently drowned and the other had to be euthanized with a gunshot."

"That was such a tragedy. So, so devastating. It was at a zoo in Hershey. Those two beautiful animals in the zoo were brother and sister; Esther was 15 and Ryan was 13. Both were born and raised there."

"Did any other zoo animals die in the flood?"

"No additional animal deaths were reported. Apparently 200 or so were taken to higher ground or evacuated. All were accounted for."

"Why weren't the two bison evacuated," Morgan said.

"They were trapped in their enclosure. The runoff from a nearby stream, Spring Creek, overwhelmed the zoo staff. The water velocity and instantaneous volume were more than they could handle."

"The small herd from northern Colorado… Are they also located near Hershey?"

"No, the wildlife park they now call home is several miles north of Hershey. I'll give more specifics after I visit the park… I want to bounce something else off of you."

"What's that?"

"You and I worked well together at the Vet Teaching Hospital."

"Yeah, we did." Morgan smiled as she flipped a ballpoint pen around with the thumb and forefinger.

"The clinic where I work is owned by a dear, dear man who opened the doors and started this practice thirty-seven years ago. I love the guy."

"That's wonderful."

"He told me yesterday evening he's going to sell the practice and retire. Asked me if I'd be interested in buying it. He'll carry the paper, even make the loan for me to purchase it."

"Wow! What an opportunity."

"I know you feel an obligation to the Navajo people to practice on the Reservation for a while—and I don't know what that length of time is—"

"Perhaps a lifetime."

"I'd love it if we could be partners, Morgan."

Morgan gazed across the open office area at the Navajo and white clients with their animals. "Britt, I am flattered beyond words. I am honored you would consider me as your partner.

But—"

"I don't need an answer now. Just tell me you'll think about it."

"I can't do that, Britt. You have to be free to find another partner. And… I'm committed to my people."

The phone line went silent for a few seconds.

"I realize that, Morgan. And I understand your commitment. They are blessed to have you."

"And, you, Britt! I am so blessed to have you in my life. I cherish our friendship and all you mean to me."

Britt laughed softly. "We better sign off before one of us starts crying." She paused. "I'll let you know what I learn about the small bison herd."

"Please take a couple of sugar cubes in your pocket."

* * *

Morgan and George enjoyed an early dinner before going to the movie, a re-release of the 1962 epic British film, *Lawrence of Arabia*. When George had asked her earlier if she would like to see the film, Morgan said, "Peter O'Toole, Omar Sharif, and that glorious music! Absolutely!"

Judging from the glances from other diners, Morgan figured they made a handsome couple. Seated at a table at Francisca's, a small family-owned restaurant in Farmington, she thought they could easily be taken as a husband and wife out for dinner.

In fact, this was their first date, alone—without her mother or his daughter. George had deposited Katie in Cynthia's care when he picked up Morgan, since his mother and father were visiting friends in Window Rock.

"My mother thinks you are a nice man," Morgan picked up

a celery stick from the small plate between them. "I don't know why, but I do, too."

He raised his eyebrows and grinned. "Some of my Army recruits would disagree with both of you." He reached for a celery stick. "I'm glad it's just the two of us tonight."

"I am, too." Morgan wore a basic black dress with a simple silver necklace and turquoise earrings. She had chosen her silver barrette to match the necklace.

He lifted his eyes. "Katie is very fond of you, Morgan. She is a good judge of people— just like her father."

"Katie is a sweetheart." She took a bite of celery. "Just like her father."

He reached for her hand. "So are you, Morgan." He reddened and looked at his watch. "We should probably order dinner so we're not late to see Peter and Omar!"

There were only a few empty seats at the Allen Movie Theater on East Main Street as the lights dimmed and the Dolby sound system gently surrounded them with the magnificent musical theme. George reached across to Morgan and took her hand as the screen came to life. She wrapped his hand in both of hers.

Chapter 18

When the screen on Britt Jennison's GPS unit went blank, she quickly pulled off the highway and stopped, then reached for the Pennsylvania road map in the glove compartment. She wasn't lost, she kept telling herself, just temporarily disoriented in an unfamiliar area of Pennsylvania!

Driving from Philadelphia to Harrisburg was a piece of cake. Heading north from Harrisburg along the Susquehanna River was delicious—the scenery, the flavor of Appalachia, and the CD music of her all-time favorite opera, Pagliacci. With the window down and the moist air blowing through her hair to somewhere in the back seat, she lost track of place and time.

Britt had left the clinic office early in the day during a light drizzle, when Philly's Friday traffic was light. Several days had passed since she and Morgan spoke on the telephone about the bison herd from northern Colorado and the young bull named Shiwana.

She unfolded the map and rested it against the steering wheel, then traced her journey from Philadelphia to Harrisburg on Interstate 76, north on US 22, exit at Dauphin to Halifax.

"Okay, Britt, so far so good," she muttered. She looked outside. The drizzle had softened, returning to mist. Traffic was intermittent; with only an occasional swoosh on her left from a passing car. She looked ahead, across the top of the steering wheel, at a highway sign. Pennsylvania Road 225 then glanced back at the map and smiled a satisfied smile. No need to be embarrassed or chagrined. She was right on track and almost on schedule to meet the manager of Frontier Wilderness Park, David Cartwright.

She folded the map and turned the ignition. When she moved forward to ease back on the highway, she saw, to her right, against a lush green hillside, several dark-haired animals and stopped again. The animals appeared to be a grazing herd of cattle. But they weren't cattle. They were the buffalo herd! She estimated twelve or fifteen of them. She had been parked right beside the wilderness park, right before her very eyes. With a mix of excitement and anticipation, she continued back onto Highway 225 to search for the park entrance.

* * *

Britt was glad to meet David Cartwright, a rugged looking guy, six feet tall, slightly heavy, dark hair, three-day growth of beard, muddy boots and work clothes—a man who apparently put his heart into his work and seemed to enjoy it.

"So you're the vet from Philadelphia? Coming to see the bison herd?" He smiled. "I didn't expect someone as young and attractive." He chuckled, took off his Philadelphia Eagles baseball cap, and scratched his head.

Britt had chosen to wear a long-sleeve blue shirt with button-down collar, khaki cargo pants and heavy leather work shoes. She sported her CSU baseball cap, while black leather work gloves dangled out of a back pocket. Around her neck hung a camera with a telephoto lens. In one of the large pockets of her cargo pants she carried a small pair of binoculars. "That's who I am, Mr. Cartwright, the veterinarian from Philadelphia." She smiled and looked around his Quonset hut office. "You've got quite a reputation in this part of the woods."

Cartwright frowned. "What do you mean?"

"You take good care of your animals here at Frontier Wilderness Park. And you've got an eye for the ladies."

"Where did you hear that?" He frowned.

"I telephoned a friend in the central part of the state for some background information and directions. He clued me in."

He folded his arms against his chest and smiled. "I love animals. Always have… And what's wrong with having an eye for good-looking ladies?"

"Not a thing. What does Mrs. Cartwright think about it?"

His eyes narrowed. "Not that it's any of your business, Miss Veterinarian from Philadelphia, but there is no Mrs. Cartwright. We were divorced seven years ago. She married a banker."

"Bad news, those bankers." Britt looked toward the open office door. "Can I visit the buffalo herd?"

"You mean the bison herd?" His question was terse.

"I mean the bison herd."

"I'll drive you out there." There was still an edge to his voice. He rubbed his chin. "But I don't want you to spook any of them. They are part of the wilderness park and they are there for people to see—from a distance. I don't want 'em to get used to humans." He turned. "Do you understand?"

"I understand." Britt patted the camera. "That's why I brought a camera with a long range lens."

"Taking pictures for yourself?"

"More for a veterinarian classmate in New Mexico. She's familiar with this herd."

"Is that right?"

"They were cared for at Colorado State, where we were in vet school."

"I'll be damned." He softened his tone. "That's interesting. They are healthy, strong animals." He walked to the door. "Let's get in the truck. It's about three-quarters of a mile out to where we can see the herd."

Britt scanned the wilderness area operation as they drove from the cluster of structures with signs directing visitors to buildings with birds, reptiles, water creatures and animals from Asia. They drove by open enclosures with a variety of animals – zebras, a couple of camels, an ostrich, and an alpaca. "You have quite a mix of animals here."

Cartwright grinned. "They keep me busy, that's for sure. But I've got a great staff."

"I appreciate your setting aside this time for my visit."

"Actually, Doc, I'm going to have to leave you on your own up here."

Britt shifted sideways in her seat.

"We have a busload of kids coming in from Harrisburg and my tour guide is sick." He shifted gears to climb a small hill. "You're looking at the backup tour guide."

As they crested the small hill, Britt spotted the bison herd in the near distance ahead of them. With the rolling hills and rain-freshened grass, it was a scene a landscape artist would die for.

He pointed. "There they are, Doc." He slowed the truck and stopped but kept the engine running. "Again, I apologize for leaving you alone out here." He gazed ahead and squinted. "See that big boulder up ahead poking out of the grass?"

Britt followed his line of sight. "I see it."

"Don't go beyond that. I don't want you getting too close and alarming the herd."

"Understand."

"Stay out here as long as you want. You'll be able to study those critters with that long-range lens you've got. Or your binoculars."

"Okay."

"It's not all that far back to my Quonset hut. Can you walk that without a problem?"

Britt laughed. "Many times over, Mr. Cartwright. Many times over." She opened the truck door and stepped down. "I'll be fine. I'll take a few camera shots and head on back."

"Good luck."

Britt walked down the grassy slope to the boulder. The low rumbling roar from the muffler on Cartwright's truck was the only sound intruding on the peaceful setting.

The boulder was rounded at the top like a huge river rock. It protruded three or four feet above the surface of the ground and provided an excellent spot for Britt to sit and observe the bison herd mid-way across the spacious green meadow. She sat with her heavy work shoes resting on the ground and retrieved the binoculars from a deep cargo pants pocket. She removed the lens caps, and adjusted the range.

Her spine tingled as she counted one large older bull, seven cows, a couple of younger bulls, and three or four calves with their rust red hair. She suspected one of the young bulls was Shiwana but she wasn't certain.

"Wow!" She set the binoculars on the boulder and lifted the camera. She removed the cap from the long lens and adjusted the eyepiece.

Britt took a half-dozen shots. *Click, whir. Click, whir. Click, whir.* Then lowered the camera to rest for a moment. She removed her green baseball cap and shook her head; her shoulder-length light brown hair rising then gently resting again. She closed her eyes and breathed deeply.

In the distance a meadowlark sang to its mate. An Eastern Meadowlark! A rare and beautiful bird.

She picked up the binoculars and searched in the direction of the birdsong. A flash of yellow caught her eye. She panned back slowly. There he sat, perched on a fencepost, singing his heart out.

Then, as quickly as she found him, he flew away. "Damn!"

Britt returned to the bison and studied the young bulls. The one closest to her lifted his head and looked in her direction. And she saw it! The small white cloud beneath his left eye. She had found Shiwana!

She set down the binoculars and picked up the camera. Shiwana stood, looking in her direction. *Click, whir. Click, whir. Click, whir.*

She lowered the camera. "Wonderful, wonderful, wonderful!"

Britt remained standing against the rounded boulder to observe her herd. Most of the herd ignored her. Only Shiwana looked up at her from time to time.

After thirty minutes and a few more camera shots, she stood, reached into another pocket, and pulled out three sugar cubes. She held them up in the air and looked toward the herd.

Shiwana had been grazing near the front of the herd. He lifted his head again and gazed at Britt.

"Shiwana," Britt called in a low voice, "These are for you. They are from Morgan."

She set the three white sugar cubes on the boulder where she had been sitting and turned to walk back to David Cartwright's office.

When she reached the crest of the hill, she glimpsed back. Shiwana was still watching her. She started down the other side and began the half-mile walk. She had covered a short distance when she heard the low rumbling roar from the muffler of Cartwright's truck. She looked up to see the pickup approaching across the open, grassy terrain.

Cartwright did a wide U-turn and pulled up beside her. "Hop in. I'll take you on back." His left elbow rested on the open window frame.

"I thought you were with the Harrisburg school kids."

"They cancelled the trip because of rain in Harrisburg." He grinned. "Hop in."

Britt walked around the back of the pickup and climbed in the passenger side. "I took some remarkable camera shots."

He released the brakes and shifted gears. "That's good. I'm glad it worked out." Cartwright drove a short distance down the two-rutted path and, instead of continuing ahead to his office, he turned left to another building set back from the others.

"Where are we going?"

He nodded toward the small log cabin structure. "Thought I'd show you where I live."

"I really need to get on back to Philadelphia." Britt's gut tightened. "It will be dark by the time I get on the interstate at Harrisburg."

"This will just take a minute." They pulled up in front of the cottage and stopped. Cartwright turned off the engine and opened his door. "Come on in."

Britt glanced to her right at the other Frontier Wilderness Park buildings about 300 yards away. Her white Subaru

Outback was parked beside the Quonset hut office. She turned. "I really need to get on the road." Her heart beat faster against the camera resting on her chest.

He climbed down and walked around the pickup. He opened her door and stepped back. "Come on."

Britt remained seated and stared at him. "Are you hard of hearing, Mr. Cartwright?"

"Let's go inside and have some fun." He placed his hand on her knee and glanced at her chest. "You can drive home in the morning."

Britt grabbed his wrist. "Go take a cold shower."

Cartwright grinned.

"Now."

He dropped his hand.

She got out of the truck. "I'm walking down to my car by myself." Her heart thumped faster as beads of sweat formed on her forehead and beneath her armpits. Her mouth went dry.

He stepped back. "I'm sorry, Doc." His face lost its color. "I didn't mean it that way."

Britt didn't move.

"I really didn't." He extended his hand. "I'm sorry."

"Hasta la vista, Mr. Cartwright." She pivoted and strode to her car.

* * *

David Cartwright stood, ashen-faced, watching the young veterinarian from Philadelphia escape his charm and drive away from Frontier Wilderness Park.

* * *

Three-quarters of a mile to the north, Shiwana walked to the rounded boulder and sniffed the white cubes left by Britt. He picked them up with his large pink tongue and raised his head searching in the direction she had gone.

He remained there until darkness fell. Then he returned to the herd.

Chapter 19

Katie sat at the small wooden desk in her bedroom studying the newspaper photograph of Miss Indian World holding her hand and Anita's. George had given her a copy of *The Navajo Times* as a souvenir of their visit to The Gathering of Nations in Albuquerque. In the photograph Morgan was standing behind Katie.

She got up from the desk and held the photo next to the camera portrait of her deceased mother, Mary, hanging on the wall. She studied the two photographs and noted a striking resemblance between Morgan and her mother. Was it her imagination—or was it a secret wish?

She was still comparing the photos when her grandmother, Lorraine Begay, knocked on her door. "I'm going to town today, Katie. Would you like to come with me and we'll find a frame for the newspaper picture?"

Katie smiled. "I'd love it, Nalí." She glanced at the photos. "I think Mom and Dr. Bluestone look like each other. Don't you?"

Lorraine stepped forward and examined the two photos. Her gray hair was neatly folded behind her head, held in place with white yarn. "You know, they do look alike. Have you mentioned this to your father?"

"No, but I think he likes Dr. Bluestone."

"You are a very perceptive young lady."

"Do you like Dr. Bluestone?"

Lorraine looked at Katie. "Very much. I think she is a beautiful person. And a very compassionate one as well." She patted Katie's back. "I truly loved Mary… your mother. We were very close."

Katie turned and wrapped her arms around Lorraine and rested her head against her shoulder. "Mom loved you, too." She looked up. "Can I drive?"

Lorraine's eyebrows shot upward and her eyes widened. "What do you mean?"

"Can I drive your truck when we go downtown?" She turned on the innocent, impish grin that was usually the winning card with her grandmother.

"You're only fourteen. You don't know how to drive, do you?"

"Dad lets me drive his truck down the driveway sometimes."

"Driving down the driveway and driving into Shiprock are two different things!"

"Dad was fourteen when he started driving. Come on, Nalí. *Please.*"

"That was a very different time, Katie. And your father was very mature for his age. When does drivers' education begin in school?"

"Next year, when I'm fifteen. How old were you when you started driving?"

"That's different. My family *needed* me to drive." She sighed. "Very well. I'll let you drive the truck from the house down to the highway. Then we'll trade places and I'll drive us to Shiprock."

Katie kissed Lorraine on her cheek. "You're the best grandmother in the whole Navajo Nation!"

"You always say that." She turned. "I'll go get my things."

Katie saw a hint of a grin as her grandmother walked to the kitchen.

* * *

Lorraine's maroon Toyota Tacoma came to a slow stop fifty feet from the two-lane asphalt highway. Katie shifted to park, engaged the emergency brake, and turned off the engine. She wore a Shiprock High School Chieftains T-shirt. "OK, Nalí. Your turn." She opened the driver's side door.

Lorraine looked ahead, then to the left and to the right. "Just a moment." It was mid-morning. A Saturday. She breathed in the surrounding landscape of the immense Navajo Nation; the gentle outlines of ridges and distant mountains, their different shades of blue. To their left was the town of Shiprock. To their right, the blacktop highway looked like a ribbon the spirits had carefully placed on the ground as sort of an invitation. There was very little traffic.

"Katie?"

"Yes, Nalí." She turned.

"Do you feel comfortable driving this truck?"

"Yes." She placed her hands on the steering wheel and inhaled. "Very comfortable."

Lorraine was silent as she studied the highway for another few moments. "If I let you drive to get more experience and to learn, will you listen to me and do everything I tell you to do?"

Katie's face broke into a wide smile. "Yes, I will. I promise." She pulled the door closed and tightened her seatbelt.

"The best way to learn and to grow is by doing." Lorraine glanced toward the highway. "I have trust in you."

"What will my dad say?"

"I know how to handle your father."

Katie reached forward and turned the ignition.

"All right, child." Lorraine looked to her left and then to her right. "There is no traffic." She nodded to their front. "Drive this short distance to the highway and stop. Look both ways and turn to the right. Stay in the right lane, and slowly increase your speed."

Katie gripped the steering wheel with an ecstatic grin. "Okay."

Lorraine folded her hands on her lap and looked straight ahead. "Release the brake, Katie. Let's go."

Katie eased the Tacoma forward to the highway, stopped, looked to her left and to her right, stepped on the accelerator, over-turned to the right sending the right front tire off the asphalt, over-correcting to the left, crossing into the left lane, turning back, beginning to perspire, tightening her grip on the steering wheel, letting up on the gas, then pressing the accelerator to the floor, muttering "Shit!," easing back and biting her lower lip.

"Relax, child."

Katie inhaled, loosened her grip, and exhaled while the pickup stabilized, and continued forward between the white line to her left and the highway's edge to her right.

A car appeared without warning in the left lane, coming toward them from the rise a short distance away.

"Relax."

Her mouth became dry as the car came closer and faster. She steered to the right, both right wheels were in the sand and gravel. She could see dust in the rearview mirror. The car passed to her left in a blur.

"You're doing fine, Katie."

Sweat dripped down her chest and beneath her arms. She relaxed again and took a deep breath.

The pickup was holding true up the small rise. They crested the hill and looked ahead at miles and miles of rolling hills. Katie focused on the highway while Lorraine observed a couple of horses and a burro to her right and a small herd of cattle behind them. White cauliflower thunderheads were forming on the distant horizon. "What a beautiful day."

In the distance, an 18-wheeler came toward them.

"Katie, I want you to relax and pay attention to that truck up ahead," Lorraine said. "When we pass each other, you will feel a sudden gust of wind. Don't be alarmed. Just concentrate on staying in our lane. Okay?"

"Okay."

"And slow down now, just to play safe."

The semi came closer.

"Hold it steady."

"The truck is so big!"

"You're doing fine. Hold it steady."

With a swoosh and a back-draft, it was gone.

"Good work, child. Good work."

"Whew," Katie sighed. "That was scary."

Lorraine reached over and patted her knee.

They had driven about ten miles since they left the house. In the distance, Lorraine saw a familiar gas station and convenience store. "Feel like something cool to drink?"

"Yes. My mouth is so dry. It's like paper."

"Slow down and we'll ease into that gas station and get something at the convenience store."

Only a couple of customers waited inside the store and two

vehicles at the gas pumps. One was a sagging rusted Pontiac station wagon with suitcases strapped on top and the other was a pickup.

"I don't want to try to park between those cars in front of the store, Nali."

"You can park in that open are next to the barbed wire fence." Lorraine pointed to the area to their left.

"Okay."

Katie turned off the engine and she and Lorraine walked toward the entrance.

Suddenly, from the gasoline pump area to their right, a child screamed. A shrill, screeching, chilling scream! They both whirled around. A terrified little girl held the black gasoline hose, gushing gasoline up at the sky. She dropped the hose and stood, dripping with gasoline and screaming.

A cowboy at the adjacent pump disengaged the hose from his truck and dashed to the toddler, flipped the switch off on her gasoline hose and picked her up in his arms. He ran to the convenience store and shouted, "Someone call 911! We need a paramedic! *Now!*"

From behind the child's car, a long-haired, unshaven man stumbled after the cowboy yelling, "Stop! That's my daughter!" He tripped over the concrete island and fell to the ground.

Lorraine reached for Katie's arm. "Go help the man with the little girl! I'll help her father."

* * *

Katie ran and opened the glass door to the convenience store. Inside the store, the cowboy, skinny as a rail, mid-forties, held the hysterical little girl in his arms and shouted to the store clerk, "Where is the restroom?"

The clerk pointed to a narrow hallway to his right. He turned and, with Katie following him, pushed the ladies room door open while the child screamed and cry in terror-stricken fear.

"Go tell the clerk to shut down all the pumps," the cowboy called to Katie, "and to get that gasoline cleaned up out there immediately, so there's not a fire!"

Katie ran to the front of the store.

"And get the tribal police out here!" he shouted.

Lorraine and the child's father arrived, breathing heavily. The cowboy stepped aside and the father knelt on the small restroom floor with the child who stood drenched in gasoline and shivering. He tore the clothing off her skinny body as Lorraine grabbed a handful of paper towels. Together they wiped the gasoline from the girl's body and hair.

"This dear child. Dip some more towels in warm water and hand me some soap," Lorraine said to the father.

He ran water over more towels in the grimy sink. "Is that your daughter with you?"

"She's my granddaughter."

The girl cried. "I want my mommy!"

"Where is your mommy?" Lorraine said as she wiped fuel from the girl's legs.

"She's in the car," she cried, "sleeping."

"Where do you live?"

"In the car. We used to live in a house," she sobbed.

"I thought I told you not to play with that gasoline hose," the father scolded, leaning close enough for Lorraine to smell his cigarette breath. He tossed a handful of soiled towels in the restroom trashcan.

A siren approached the station.

While Lorraine dried the little girl, the cowboy, standing in the doorway, removed his pearl-buttoned cotton shirt and handed it to her. She wrapped it around the girl and cradled her in her arms.

"Thanks," the father mumbled.

"Let me through!" A paramedic shouted and entered the small space with his medical pack. "Please stay here with me, ma'am," he told Lorraine.

The father grew silent. He stepped back as the paramedic took the child's vital signs while Lorraine held her.

* * *

Katie waited inside near the cash register, watching the clerk, a middle-aged Navajo woman, as she struggled to mop up the spilled gasoline. Soon, a second patrol car, its siren shutting down to abrupt silence, drove up and a tribal policeman from the Navajo Nation Police entered the store. Outside, a second paramedic pulled a gurney from the back of an ambulance. The cowboy left the crowded restroom and walked outside bare-chested.

When the way was clear, Katie darted down the hallway to help her grandmother.

The paramedic looked up when she entered. "Young lady, would you gather these paper towels and toss them in the wastebasket and get it outside? Quickly!"

Katie filled the wastebasket with the fuel-saturated paper and carried it outside to a spot far from the building. She ran back inside as the paramedic talked to Lorraine. "The child is comfortable with you holding her."

Lorraine nodded. "She seems to be. She's stopped crying."

"Can I get anything for you? You must be tired."

"My granddaughter and I would love something to drink. That's why we stopped here."

"I'll get each of you a cold bottle of water from the ambulance when we go outside." He glanced at the little girl, then at Lorraine. "Are you a relative?"

Lorraine nodded at the father leaning against the wall.

"I'm her father."

The paramedic looked at the defeated father, then back at Lorraine. "Would you be able to carry her outside, ma'am?"

Lorraine smiled. "Young man, I've been carrying youngsters all my adult life." She placed a hand on his shoulder and stood with the child cradled in her other arm. She jerked her head toward Katie. "Including this one. Huh, Katie?"

Katie nodded.

When they exited the convenience store, Lorraine set the girl down on the convenience store sidewalk. The cowboy's shirt fit her like an oversized nightgown. As soon as her bare feet touched the concrete surface, she ran to her mother. "Mommy!"

The paramedic brought Lorraine and Katie each a cold bottle of water. As they wet their dry throats, Katie observed the tribal policeman calling in a report to Dispatch while the second paramedic questioned the girl's mother, who sprawled in the cluttered back seat of the old Pontiac. Her hair was dirty and matted; she appeared to be in a daze.

Someone had spread sand and dirt on the concrete beside the pumps to soak up the spilled gasoline.

The cowboy strode to his pickup parked beside the gas

pump and retrieved a Levi jacket from behind the front seat. He put it on and walked back to Lorraine and Katie. The hair on his chest was curlier and a lighter brown than the hair on his head. "This was quite an experience!"

"Yes it was." Lorraine shook her head.

The cowboy tipped his hat. "My name is Matt Carmody. Thanks for helping me, ma'am."

Lorraine smiled. "You're welcome, Mr. Carmody. I am Lorraine Begay and this is my granddaughter, Katie."

The tribal cop completed his report, then walked over to Lorraine. "Thank you for your help. I have someone from our family services office in Shiprock coming over."

Lorraine nodded to the officer. "My granddaughter and I will leave now."

He stepped back and Lorraine and Katie walked toward their Tacoma. They had taken only a few steps when Lorraine took out a small coin purse from a skirt pocket.

Katie watched as her grandmother pulled out a twenty-dollar bill and walked to the girl's mother. She handed the bill to the woman. "Go inside and get your family some food to eat."

When they arrived at the truck, Lorraine turned to Katie. "Okay if I drive us back?"

"Yes Nalí." She handed her grandmother the keys.

They drove a few miles in silence when Katie said, "Will the little girl recover?"

"I think so, Katie. It may be difficult for her, but I think she'll be all right." She glanced at Katie. "What we just saw, you and I, was a page out of life. One never knows what might happen. We must count our blessings."

"I know." Katie stared down at her hands folded on her lap.

"I'll get a frame for the newspaper picture on Monday."

"Thank you, Nalí. I don't feel like going to town today."

What is life?
It is the flash of a firefly in the night.
It is the breath of a buffalo in the wintertime.
It is the little shadow which runs across the grass and
loses itself in the sunset.

Crowfoot (1821-1890)
Blackfoot warrior and chief

MONTANA

Chapter 20

On a midweek morning, things in the clinic were running at a steady pace. Morgan dealt with an even flow of appointments and walk-ins, including the fitting of a fiberglass cast on the rear leg of a sheep dog injured when his leg got caught in a cattle guard. The procedure she followed was identical to the one she conducted on the German shepherd in Dr. Bourland's class her third year in vet school. When she was finished she ran her fingers through the fur behind the sheep dog's ears and thought of Jimmy Castle, hoping he was well in his Grand Junction practice.

Cynthia handled most of the telephone calls and Garrison kept busy caring for the boarding animals in the clinic as well as two horses and an injured ewe in the corrals behind the clinic building.

Morgan sat at her desk and wrote a prescription for a rancher's aging border collie. She handed it to him with verbal instructions on its application. Then she glanced through the morning mail. There were envelopes from both Suki and Britt!

"Wow!" she said as she reached for the shiny metal letter opener with its Colorado State University handle.

She opened the large brown envelope first. The return address, in bold print, read: **Suki Winters, Doctor of Veterinary Medicine, Bozeman, Montana**. Inside was a handwritten letter from Suki along with paper-clipped sections taken from newspapers and magazines.

Hi Kiddo,

I hope you are enjoying good health – and that your practice is going like gangbusters. I think of you so often and of the fun we had during our undergrad years and vet school. We worked hard and we played hard. (Sometimes Suki played too hard!)

Remember when we accompanied the herd of buffalo from Yellowstone to the Fort Peck Reservation? And the photo of me flipping a bird at that jerk with the thick glasses? What a moron! That was a real ornery bunch. None has become clients of mine, by the way. Their brucellosis fears are pretty shallow.

The reason I'm writing is to ask if your schedule might permit a visit to Montana in a couple of weeks. The tribes are having an anniversary celebration of the buffalo herd's arrival at Fort Peck. My dad ran into one of the tribal elders who told him of the gathering and hopes we might be there. Dad didn't want to tell me for fear of our safety.

I think the tribal elders would love it if "the Kewa sisters" could join them. I'll also write to Brittany to see if she can break away from Philadelphia to be with us. Sort of a reunion for the three of us.

Miss you lots,
Suki

Morgan leafed through the articles enclosed with Suki's letter. The newspaper clippings were from a Billings newspaper and the magazine articles contained color photographs of buffalo as well as interviews with elders from the Sioux and Assiniboine tribes. She read the items then pulled a note pad across the desk and wrote, *Ayani*, the Navajo word for buffalo. "You ayani at Fort Peck; you have made us proud," she said in a soft voice.

She remembered Teetonka, the Sioux tribal elder, and his

genuine gratitude. "The arrival of these buffalo has deep spiritual meaning for us," he had said as he reached for Suki's hand and hers. She could still feel the touch of his calloused, working hand against hers.

Then she picked up the smaller, but thicker, envelope from Britt.

My Dear Morgan,
(You can't look at the enclosed snapshots until you read this note!)

Guess what? I found Shiwana! I found your cloud spirit, Shiwana. And he is a magnificent animal!

Last Friday, I took the day off from the clinic and drove to the Frontier Wilderness Park in the central part of Pennsylvania. It is a top-notch facility where the animals are very well cared for. The park manager is pretty full of himself, but he is taking good care of Shiwana and the herd—that is what's important.

The herd has increased in size from the eight we knew in Fort Collins to fifteen today. The calves are precious. And Shiwana is a handsome young bull. You'll see in the photos.

Suki wrote and invited me to join the two of you at the Fort Peck Reservation in Montana for the commemoration ceremonies of the bison herd you guys helped deliver several years ago. Unfortunately, time and distance won't allow me to make the trip. Maybe next time. If Suki throws a finger and gets her picture in the newspapers again, please send me a copy.

Seriously, though, you two be careful, okay? There are still people out there who can be dangerous.

Give my love to your mom.

Love to you too, my dearest friend,
Britt

Morgan opened a smaller envelope containing the color photographs and examined them one by one. She held her breath when she came to the photo of Shiwana looking directly at the camera. He had, indeed, become an exquisite animal.

She reached for a magnifying glass and held the photograph beneath the desk lamp to examine it more closely. The white cloud beneath his left eye had not changed. She smiled, immersed in the memories of that misty morning in Fort Collins when she glimpsed outside from her apartment window and saw the buffalo calf with his reddish tan fur, grazing beside a large aspen and his stopping to look up and their eyes made contact.

And now, seated at the desk in her Four Corners clinic, she held the photograph of a husky young bull.

Her hands had gripped the black plastic handle of the curved magnifying glass for several moments when she sensed a hand resting on her shoulder.

"Are we daydreaming?" Cynthia said. "Or studying something?"

"It's like Christmas, Mother! A wonderful letter from Suki and beautiful photographs from Britt. Photos of Shiwana. Look!" She held up a photo of the young buffalo bull. "Do you think Suki and Britt would like George?"

"I'm sure they would, Morgan, but we can talk about that later." She turned her head toward the clients and pets in the waiting area.

"I guess I do have a clinic with patients waiting to see me—"

"Yes, you do, and one of the clients is Henry Lewis. He has an ailing burro with a bad leg abscess. He's quite worried. I'll look at Britt's photos later."

"I apologize for spacing out." Morgan stood and grabbed

her stethoscope from the desk. "Is the burro in the holding pen?"

"Yes. Garrison is back there with Mr. Lewis. He got the burro for his granddaughter for her birthday."

"Can you take care of things in here while I go examine him?"

"Of course." Cynthia patted Morgan on her arm and walked to the front desk.

Morgan proceeded down the narrow hallway to the back door. Ever since that first day when Henry Lewis walked thru her door, he occupied a special place in Morgan's veterinary practice. She liked the man. He could be abrupt and sometimes bordered on rude, but you always knew where you stood with Henry and you could trust his every word.

She opened the back door. A coconut brown burro on the other side of the holding pen waited while Garrison Greyeyes knelt beside him to examine his leg. Behind Garrison stood Lewis and a little girl, ten or twelve years old.

"Good morning, Doc," Lewis held out his hand to Morgan. "This is my granddaughter, Henrietta." He nodded down at the little girl. "And her donkey, Chico."

"Hi, Henrietta." Morgan smiled at the child. "Are you named for your grandfather?"

"Uh-huh." The girl nodded.

"And do you know the Spanish name for donkey?"

"Burro!" Henrietta almost shouted.

"That's right!" Morgan laughed.

She turned and patted Chico, then knelt beside Garrison. "What have you found?"

Garrison held the animal's back leg. "A badly abscessed wound. He got tangled up in some barbed wire. Goddamned barbed wire!" He shook his head.

Chico turned his head and looked back. He swished his tail with its short hair and tuft at the end and threw his large furry ears forward as though he was a participant in the conversation.

Morgan examined the wound. "We need to drain that abscess. Run to my office and get my medical bag. It's got everything I'll need."

Garrison ran across the holding pen and dashed inside.

Morgan studied the wound closer. It was on the outside of the burro's left rear leg. "He may be experiencing a lot of pain, but we'll take care of it." She spoke to Henry Lewis and Henrietta as well as to herself.

"He doesn't seem to be showing any pain though, Doc." Henry said.

"Burros are tough little guys, Henry. Horses sometimes raise a real fuss when they're in pain. Burros seem to internalize it, which can make it challenging for a vet to diagnose their problem."

She put on her glasses and pressed the area around the wound. "I'll drain this, clean it, apply medication, and wrap it. It won't take long. Then it is up to Henrietta to change the dressing and apply lots of TLC." She turned. "Can you do all that for me? And for Chico?"

Henrietta's shiny black hair was tied in pigtails. And she wore a cowboy hat just like her grandfather's. She nodded a serious nod. "Yes, ma'am."

"Is that okay with you, Mr. Lewis?"

"It sure is." He looked down at Henrietta's. "Now you pay attention, honey, to what Dr. Bluestone is doing."

"Yes, Grandpa."

"You know, Henrietta," Morgan got down on her knees as

she placed her arm around the child's narrow waist. "Burros' legs are very dainty and slender. The loads these little legs have carried over thousands of years are beyond my imagination. Horses are bigger and they are faster, but they don't have the endurance or the patience of a donkey." She reached up and patted Chico just as Garrison arrived with the MedPac.

He opened the MedPac and placed it on the ground beside Morgan.

"Thanks, Garrison." She reached inside and grabbed a bottle of sterile saline solution. "Are you strong enough to watch this, Henrietta?"

"Yes, ma'am."

"If it bothers you, you don't have to look."

Henrietta stood at Morgan's shoulder. "I'll be fine."

Chico gazed back at Morgan again, with his large ears forward, as if to assure her that he, too, would be okay.

Morgan lanced the abscess, releasing additional pus. The burro flinched and his leg muscle tightened for a kick. She kept talking to him and petting him. Then she flushed the wound with the saline solution. "This isn't as bad as I thought it would be."

She handed the saline bottle to Garrison then dabbed the wound with sterile gauze. She studied the wound. "Now, Henrietta, this is where I want you to pay attention."

She glimpsed up at Lewis, who wore his stained summer Stetson. The old rancher nodded.

Morgan held her hand out to Garrison, who placed a tube of ointment in her palm. "This is an antibiotic ointment. I'm going to give you this tube to take home." Morgan applied the ointment to the five-centimeter wound, while the girl watched without moving. She capped the tube and handed it to Henrietta. Then she applied a bandage over the wound. "Garrison, make sure Henrietta gets a supply of these bandages to take with her."

"Will do, Doctor."

Then Morgan wrapped the leg with heavy gauze and held it in place with adhesive tape. "I can see you and your granddad are closely following every step. So I want you to change Chico's dressing every day."

Henrietta was wide-eyed. She nodded. "I can do that."

"I'll drive out to your place a week from today and we'll see how Chico is doing. If there is a problem before then, you or your grandfather call me."

Henrietta patted her donkey. "Yes, ma'am."

Morgan stood and put her arm over Chico's neck. With her other hand she rubbed his forehead and his ears. "Chico," she said, "you and Henrietta are going to travel many days and many miles together and the spirits are going to care for both of you." She turned and shook hands with Henry Lewis and Henrietta.

"Thanks, Doc," he said. "And I must tell you that my fore-man, Terrill Lee, took a shine to you when you came out to help Rusty deliver her foal. He asked me to give you his regards."

"Thank you, Henry. I love what I do." She patted Chico's cheek. "Please give my best wishes to Mr. Lee."

Henry Lewis pulled his leather gloves from his back pocket. "Let's load Chico on the trailer, honey."

Morgan felt Chico's eyes on her as she walked across the holding pen to the clinic, until she entered the building and the door closed behind her.

Chapter 21

Morgan and George spent more of their free time together and at social gatherings or tribal get-togethers were often assumed to be a married couple. George's parents, Lorraine and Winston, had also grown fond of Morgan.

"My dad loves to play Navajo string games." George told her one evening on their way back to his house. "He's waiting to challenge you."

"What are those?"

"He takes a loop of string and with his hands creates different figures, such as coyotes, birds, stars, and many other designs."

"Sounds intriguing." Morgan wondered if her father had ever learned to play such games.

"By tradition, the games can be played only during the winter season—otherwise the player will fall off a horse, be struck by lightning, or be pissed on by spiders." George laughed as he held the front door open for Morgan.

"Ah, Morgan," Winston called from across the room. "Come join me at the kitchen table. I have something to show you."

"Waste of time, I warn you," said Lorraine with a smirk.

When Morgan caught on after only a few rounds, George said with pride in his voice, "Didn't I tell you? She's got the fingers of a surgeon. She is a natural."

Morgan grinned at father and son. "I look forward to many challenging evenings like this."

* * *

Winston, with another Navajo partner, had established a small home and business security company in Shiprock. Late one afternoon, George dropped by his father's business on his way home from the livestock supply store in Farmington.

"So, when are you going to ask Morgan to marry you?" Winston growled. He tinkered with a home security device at his workbench.

"What do you mean?"

"You two spend so much time together, you should be married." Winston, stocky, solid, and grey-haired, was shorter than George. He raised his eyebrows. "You want me to ask her for you?"

"No, thank you, Dad." George laughed.

"You still miss Mary?"

"No, that's not it." He folded his arms across his chest. "I'll always miss Mary."

"Hand me that Phillips screwdriver. Your combat injuries bothering you?"

"My insides are pretty messed up. But everything still works, if that's what you mean." He grinned.

Winston nodded. He hummed and tinkered some more. Then he placed his hands on the workbench and sat up. "George, if you don't ask her, someone else will. Morgan is a very attractive woman."

"What about Katie?"

"Katie adores Morgan!" He shook his head. "Haven't you

noticed? You Army guys are smart as hell about being warriors and shooting guns, but sometimes you are a little slow about other things in life."

* * *

A few nights later, Morgan and Cynthia invited George and Katie to a casual spaghetti dinner at their rental home outside Shiprock.

"I want to ask George to go to Fort Peck with me," Morgan said to her mother as they prepared dinner. "I told Suki I would go with her. We would feel better if George came with us."

"I'll worry about you anyway," Cynthia said.

* * *

From a few miles west, Katie and George drove to the spaghetti dinner with Airborne in the back seat of the pickup. Katie liked being with Morgan and Cynthia. Their house was like a second home.

"After dinner, you can do your homework at the kitchen table while the adults go to the living room to visit," George said.

"I want to be in the living room, too. I'll be quiet."

"But that won't get your homework done, will it?"

She shook her head.

"Okay?"

She looked up and grinned at her father. "I'll make you a deal. Can we go to the Shiprock Chieftain's basketball game next Friday?"

"Why? You just want to look at those cute guys, huh?" He

poked her in the ribs.

Katie's face turned red with a bashful grin.

"We'll go to the basketball game." He reached across the seat and tussled her hair. "And after dinner, you and Airborne stay in the kitchen and do your homework."

"Deal."

* * *

"Have you ever been to Montana?" Morgan asked George as she dropped the dry spaghetti stems into the boiling water and stirred. The silver and turquoise bracelet given to her by her grandmother shone against her light brown skin.

"Went fishing near Bozeman with an Army buddy one time." George sat with Cynthia at the kitchen table. Airborne was curled up at his feet. He took a sip from his can of Miller Lite. "Why?"

"Want to come with Suki Winters and me to the Fort Peck Indian Reservation? Up near the Canadian border?"

"That sounds like a fun trip. What's the occasion?"

Cynthia winked at him. "Morgan wants someone else to do the driving, so she can enjoy the scenery."

Katie stood with her back to Morgan, slicing tomatoes and lettuce on the wooden cutting board beside the sink.

Morgan turned down the gas on the stove when the water began to boil. "Suki is my old vet school roommate, and we've been invited by the Sioux and Assiniboine tribes to join them in a celebration of their buffalo herd."

"It was you and Suki who got into trouble years ago when the original herd was trucked up there from Yellowstone, wasn't it?"

"That's right." She stirred the spaghetti. "You didn't know I used to be an agitator, did you?" She laughed. "That's what they actually called us. Agitators! In the newspaper! We couldn't believe it."

"When I was stationed at Fort Lewis, I remember reading about some people in Montana getting bent out of shape by a herd of buffalo and a couple of college kids. Didn't expect to be sitting in a kitchen with one of them tonight." He reached for some potato chips. "You and Suki better be careful. Those guys might be looking for the two of you."

"That's why I want you to come." Morgan stood holding the long wooden spoon in the pan. "Things might get nasty. I'd like it if you were there."

Cynthia looked up. "I would too, George."

"When is this Fort Peck gathering taking place?"

"Two weeks from today," Morgan said. "And it will probably take a couple of days to drive up there."

"From what I've read, the cattle ranchers still have more political clout than the tribes."

"They always have, George," Cynthia said. "But we are told the governor backs the tribes."

"Do you and your friend Suki know what you're getting into?"

"I feel we do. Suki and her family have been Montana farmers for generations. They don't object to what we're doing— celebrating the buffalo."

"I imagine Suki's family has experienced some resentment and anger from the cattle people." George reached for another potato chip.

"For sure they have," Morgan said. "Suki has told me of a couple of uncomfortable encounters she has had."

"George?" Cynthia said.

He looked across the kitchen table.

"I would like you to go up there with Morgan. You won't let anyone give her a hard time. She and Suki will be safe with you around."

He said nothing.

Katie kept her hands on the cutting board as she turned slightly awaiting her father's answer.

He reached across the table and patted Cynthia's arm. "You've convinced me, so I'll go."

"Thank you, George." Cynthia stood.

"There is something I would like to ask *you*, Cynthia."

"And what is that?"

"May I have your permission to ask your daughter to marry me?"

Morgan froze in mid-stir at the spaghetti pot. She stared wide-eyed at George and bit her lower lip.

Katie spun around open-mouthed, holding a tomato in one hand and a paring knife in the other.

Cynthia threw her arms in the air and laughed. She walked around the table, bent over, and kissed George on the cheek. "Permission granted!"

George stood and walked to Morgan still standing at the stove. She turned to him with an expectant grin.

"So what do you think?" He placed his index finger on her nose. "Wanna marry Katie and me?"

Her eyes danced and she threw her arms around him. "Yeah, I wanna marry you and Katie." She reached out and put an arm around Katie's waist and pulled her to them.

"Dad, you are awesome!" Katie squealed.

Airborne came out from under the kitchen table to see what was going on.

George held Morgan's face in his hands and kissed her, and then he stepped back. "We can get married before we go to Fort Peck or when we get back."

Morgan tilted her head.

"I've been checking," he continued. "There are different ways to contract for marriage on the Navajo Nation. The fastest and easiest way is to sign a Navajo Nation marriage license in front of two witnesses who also sign the license. No muss, no fuss, no fancy ceremony. It's done!"

Morgan laughed. "You *have* been doing your homework, haven't you?"

Cynthia chimed in. "I guess I could be a witness."

"And," George said, "my father will be the other witness."

"Let me be a witness, too!" Katie chimed in.

Morgan still held the wooden spaghetti spoon in her right hand. She raised it and spun around to face her mother. "How about next week? After we close the clinic Friday evening."

Cynthia smiled. "You sure you don't want a more traditional wedding? Like your father and I had?"

"And let George Henry Begay drag this out forever?" She laughed. "No thanks, Mom. The sooner the better."

George spoke up. "I don't know what you're talking about."

Morgan grinned. "I think you do, Mr. Procrastinator."

He pinched her cheek. "I'll go to the tribal office tomorrow and pick up a marriage license."

"Can I go with you, Dad?"

George winked at her. "I'll pick you up after school."

Cynthia chortled and walked to the refrigerator. She pulled

out a bottle of champagne someone had given her when she and Morgan first arrived in Shiprock from Kewa Pueblo. She placed it on the kitchen counter with three large glasses and a small one.

Then she walked to her bedroom and picked up the wedding basket from which she and Morgan's father had eaten blue corn mush on their wedding day. As she reached to turn off the bedroom light, her eye caught the photo on her nightstand of Jonathan and herself seated at the dining room table on their wedding day. He sat beside her as they both held the wedding basket, starry-eyed love written across both of their faces. She knew he would be proud again tonight. Proud of his daughter and proud to welcome George to his clan. Cynthia lifted the framed photograph and kissed it then returned it to its special place.

She returned to the kitchen and handed the basket to Morgan.

"I don't know what to say, Mother." She gazed down at the basket and her eyes shone.

George leaned forward and kissed Cynthia on the cheek. "Thank you, Cynthia."

* * *

Before she went to sleep, Katie looked up at the wall beside her bed at her own newly framed photographs of her mother and Morgan. She placed her hands on each of them. Then she turned off the light and crawled into bed.

Chapter 22

The Winters farm, 17 miles northeast of Bozeman, Montana, was 440 miles from the buffalo herd at the Fort Peck Indian Reservation. The reservation, up in the northeastern corner of the state, butted against North Dakota to the east and Canada to the north.

Suki Winters' father, Jack, had a farmer's build and a farmer's handshake; a round, friendly face and thinning hair. He wore his signature khaki pants and work shirt. He looked across the breakfast table. "George, how does it feel to be having breakfast with two doctors of veterinary medicine?"

George glanced at Morgan, seated beside him, and Suki, next to her father. Suki's mother, Maude, sat at the end of the table to his left. "Sir, I think you and I are in the company of three pretty impressive women, two of whom are vets." He nudged Morgan. "And one of them happens to be my wife."

"For a whole week!" Morgan added.

"Maude and I are delighted for both of you. But, George," he turned his breakfast fork around in his hand, "I would be less than honest with you if I let on I wasn't concerned about the three of you heading up there on your own. Some of those people aren't going to be happy to see my daughter, Suki, and your wife, Morgan. Not after the way they stirred things up several years ago."

Jack raised his eyebrows. "Did you ever see the newspaper picture of Suki?"

George nodded and grinned. "Yes sir, I did."

"Dad," Suki said, "it was those asshole demonstrators who stirred things up. Morgan and I were just standing up for the buffalo and the tribes. We were minding our own business." She patted his almost-bald head. "It was you, by the way, who taught me to throw a finger!"

He looked up from his plate. "Guess I did, didn't I?"

"It sure wasn't me!" Maude said. "I sometimes wonder about the two of you." She shook her head. "George, would you like more coffee?"

"No thank you, ma'am. We'd better be on our way. It's about a seven hour drive up to the Fort Peck Reservation."

"Where will you stay tonight?"

"Suki made reservations for us at—I think it's called The Sherman Inn." He glanced at Suki who nodded in agreement. "It's in Wolf Point. Tomorrow morning, we'll meet the tribal elders at Turtle Mound."

"That's not far from Wolf Point. About 50 miles northeast," Maude said. "I'm grateful, George, that you'll be with these two girls."

* * *

"Wolf Point, Montana, the seat of Roosevelt County, became an outpost on the Missouri River in the mid-1800s." Morgan read aloud to George from a travel brochure. "Today it is a town with a population of 2,500, 56 percent white and 41 percent Native American. Monte Montana, the famous rodeo trick rider, grew up in Wolf Point. Its mayor, Mathew Golik, died at the age of 59 when his three-wheeler went through the ice at Fort Peck Lake where he'd been ice fishing. That was on March 1, 2005. He drowned."

"They come right to the point, don't they?"

The sun approached the western horizon as George pulled into a gas station outside the town. He and Morgan were in the front seat of the gray king cab and Suki snoozed in the back seat.

When he stopped beside one of the two gas pumps, Suki sat up. "Are we there yet?"

"Yes, ma'am. Ladies room is inside to your right."

Morgan turned. "How do you know where the ladies room is?"

"Just joking." He glanced toward the door. "This place is too small to have a ladies room."

The station consisted of a cash register sitting on a display case with cigarettes and candy bars. Next to it was an open maintenance bay where an old Dodge pickup was up on the rack for an oil and lube job.

They climbed out of the truck. The ladies stretched while George gassed up. None of them paid much attention to two men emerging from the cashier's counter.

* * *

The two men were in their late twenties, early thirties. One of them, with thick glasses, wore a beat-up cowboy hat. His hair extended below his shirt collar and he was unshaven. He stood in front of the door and opened a fresh pack of cigarettes. He set his teeth against the filter tip end of one of the cigarettes and pulled it from the pack. He squinted at the two women standing beside the pickup at the gas pump. And he froze.

"What's the matter, Billy?" the other man said. He was short with a beer belly gut stretching a soiled yellow T-shirt to its max.

"Those two women. I've seen them before." Billy Fry said. He lit the cigarette and exhaled. "Can't remember just where." He pulled his hat down over his eyes and stared in their direction.

"We gotta get going, Billy."

He took another drag on his cigarette. "Just wait a goddam minute. Besides we're not going anywhere 'til they finish on the truck."

* * *

Morgan had her back to the two men. Suki faced her while they chatted. She glanced over Morgan's shoulder and stopped in mid-sentence. "Don't turn around, Morgan. The asshole with the thick glasses who gave us a hard time years ago is standing 30 feet behind you, smoking a cigarette and staring at me."

Morgan looked down at the ground and folded her arms against her chest. "The guy you flipped off?"

"That's the one."

Morgan looked beyond Suki at George. He removed the hose from the pickup's gas tank and returned it to the pump. "Want me to get George's attention?"

"Not yet."

George replaced the cap on the gas tank. "Let's get moving," he called.

Morgan looked directly at him but didn't say anything.

He glanced at her, then locked his eyes beyond her at the two men standing in front of the door. The one with thick-lensed glasses stared at Suki while the other one tugged on his arm.

"Come on, Billy. We've got to get back to unloading that lady's furniture." Billy's companion glanced at Suki and Morgan, then back at Billy.

Billy Fry spun around and yelled something at the mechanic just as the lift lowered the pickup to the ground.

"Let's get in the truck," Suki said. "Pronto."

George made sure that by the time Billy Fry paid for the oil and lube job and got on the highway, the gray king cab had disappeared. He drove a half-mile to The Sherman Inn where they checked in. Suki's room was directly across the hallway from his and Morgan's.

At dinner they discussed the suspicious man with the thick glasses and his friend.

"You're sure that was the guy who made the front page with you years ago?" George said.

"No doubt in my mind." Suki took a sip of her red wine. "I'd recognize that jerk anywhere."

"You think he recognized you and Morgan?"

"I'm not sure. He was sure working on it. Glad we drove away when we did."

"I am, too," Morgan said.

"Let's stay on alert." George motioned to the waitress. "I'm starved."

* * *

At Dad's Bar on Main Street, Billy Fry sat by himself on one end of the bar nursing another Budweiser. Two tables behind him were occupied by customers. One other person, a railroad worker, was seated at the other end of the bar.

Dad, the proprietor and bartender, wiped down the bar for

the third time in ten minutes. He stood down at the end with the railroad worker, a man everyone knew as Jake. Jake maintained a desk at the Amtrak station building on Front Street, but no one ever asked what he did. He was a supervisor of some sort and drove a company car. Sometimes he carried a briefcase; sometimes a toolbox. He was a friendly man and usually well dressed in his work clothes.

Dad propped a foot up on the railing behind the bar and leaned forward. "Busy day today, Jake?"

Jake was a husky man with a deep voice. "Yeah, I did my part to keep the wheels turning on the shiny rails. Lots of rail traffic these days." He leaned back and emptied his glass of draft beer.

"Ready for another one?"

"One more, then I'm going home."

Dad set a fresh glass of draft in front of Jake. Dad's wavy white hair was reflected in the large mirror behind the bar. Beneath the mirror were three lighted rows of liquor bottles of different shapes and colors. The jukebox music was set at a level where conversations were not easily overheard.

Jake glanced down the bar at Billy Fry. "What do you know about Billy?" he said. "I understand he's in trouble with the law again."

"That's what I hear," Dad said in a low voice. "Somebody told me he was trying to hold up a gas station over in Glasgow last week and tripped over a case of oil next to the cash register. Fell on his ass. He can't see worth a damn, even with those thick glasses." Dad suppressed a grin.

"Did they jail him?"

"He spent a day in the cooler. I hear they're trying to decide whether or not to indict him." Dad made another pass across the bar with the towel. "Some towns have their 'Town Drunk.' We have Billy Fry. God, he's always into something." He shook his head. "Wish he wouldn't come in here."

"Does he have family?"

"Not nearby. He drifted into town several years ago from California, San Francisco, I think. Family threw him out."

"Drugs?"

"That's what I understand." Dad glanced over at the tables and the customers enjoying themselves. "Some of those damn drugs can fry your brain. I'm told Billy gets a check every month so he'll stay here and not go back to California. Lives by himself in a small place a few blocks away. Drives an old Dodge pickup."

"So he doesn't hold a job?"

"Doesn't need one as long as Mom and Dad keep sending the checks. But he picks up an odd job every now and then for a few extra bucks."

Jake took a sip of beer. "Does he have any friends?"

"There's a heavyset little guy that hangs around with him sometimes. Other than that, I don't think so. The dumb bastard just gets into trouble. He's got a chip on his shoulder. If there's a protest or a fight, Billy Fry will be there. Why the hell he tried to hold up that place in Glasgow, I don't know. He was probably higher than a kite."

Dad turned and glanced at the red and green neon clock above the cash register. "Closing time is in 30 minutes. Want another one?"

Jake shook his head.

Dad placed the towel underneath the bar next to the sink and strolled around to the two tables with customers. "Gonna be closing in 30 minutes. Anybody want a refill?"

He took three beer orders and, for the almost-drunk wife of a local politician, a vodka on ice.

Dad took care of the orders and walked back to the bar. "How 'bout you, Billy? Want another one?"

Billy Fry squinted through his thick-lensed glasses. "Uh-huh."

Dad reached into the cooler for another Bud.

Billy shoved some money across the bar. "Still can't remember who the hell they are," he mumbled. "But I don't like 'em."

"You don't like who?" Dad asked.

"Two women I saw today." He belched and wiped his mouth with his shirt sleeve. "Can't remember 'em. Don't like 'em." He emptied the bottle, dropped his head onto his folded arms on the bar, and within moments was snoring like an 18-wheeler.

Chapter 23

"Welcome back, my Kewa sisters." Teetonka, the Sioux elder stood facing Morgan and Suki. His hair had become white and his thin body almost frail. "The irises of my eyes have begun to melt a little at the edges since we were last together. But I can clearly see both of your faces and the beauty you bring to our people."

He turned to George, standing beside Morgan. "George Begay, my brother, our tribes welcome you as well."

George wore his black cowboy hat. He nodded. "Thank you, Teetonka. I'm honored to be with you."

As they stood at the pasture fence, Morgan and Suki observed the herd with deeper knowledge and appreciation than they did years earlier as undergraduate students. The herd, grazing a short distance from them, had grown in size since its arrival from Yellowstone on that cold, dark winter night.

"The buffalo cared for our people for many generations," Teetonka said. "Now we care for them. They fed us and clothed us and kept us warm in winter. Then they were destroyed—except for the few who found shelter and safety in Yellowstone. The animals in this herd are, as you know, direct descendants of those sheltered few."

He looked across the 2,100 acres of grassland and the dark-haired herd. The Little Rockies rose in the background. "Thank you for being with us once again to honor them."

He reached for Morgan's hand. "Look how they have mul-tiplied since you and your Kewa sister arrived with them that night after your 500 mile journey." He raised his arms and smiled. "Look at them!"

"Gives me goose bumps," Suki said. She rested her hands on the top rail of the split rail fence. "But, they still are not totally safe from the Department of Livestock. If any buffalo get out of this enclosure, they'll likely be shot. Several have met that fate in recent years." She turned and surveyed a small assemblage of protesters near the highway. "See all those people?"

"Do you think someone hired them to demonstrate?" Morgan said.

"I'm sure they are paid demonstrators," Suki said.

"Paid by whom?"

"I don't know. Might have been cattle ranchers. They're pret-ty strong. Politically and financially." Suki paused. "Brucellosis is the basis of their arguments. It can cause a mama cow to abort her calf."

"I know," Morgan said. "But that's a pretty weak argument. Brucellosis is spread to cattle more by elk."

"Agriculture officials and cattle people seem to turn a deaf ear to that premise. They don't want buffalo grazing in Montana. Period. And they've got some of the local politicians in their back pockets."

Several dozen members of the Sioux and Assiniboine tribes mingled about, in small groups and around the pasture fence. All were gathered to celebrate the Yellowstone buffalo. Morgan was proud that she and George, members of the Navajo Nation, stood among them—along with her Kewa sister, Suki.

* * *

On the other side of the highway the handful of demonstrators were taunting and loud. One of them, rousted out of bed and hungover, was Billy Fry. He wore his long grey duster coat. The sweat ring on his cowboy hat seemed to be spreading wider. He appeared borderline nauseous, and his thick glasses were steamed over.

* * *

Two tribal policemen observed the demonstrators from their patrol car a short distance down the highway.

George Begay also took notice of the demonstrators. His arm had been draped over Morgan's shoulder until he lowered it and turned toward them when he sensed a growing silence.

From the group, fifty yards away, half the distance of a football field, Billy Fry walked toward George, Morgan, Suki, and the tribal members. He stopped midway between them and the demonstrators behind him.

"I remember who you are!" he shouted. His unshaven chin jutted forward. He stared across the open space at Suki. "Screw you, lady!"

His right arm remained inside the duster while he extended his left arm with an extended middle finger. "I give back to you what you gave to me in that newspaper picture."

He turned around awaiting support from the other demonstrators. They stared at him until one of the demonstrators yelled, "He's got a gun!"

"The crazy bastard!" someone else shouted. "Let's get the hell outa here!"

At that instant, George saw movement beneath the duster as Billy Fry raised a Winchester lever-action 30-30 and aimed toward the crowd at the buffalo fence.

The two tribal policemen jumped out of their unit. One of them hit the dirt with his pistol pointed at Billy Fry. He fired one round and missed. The other ran toward Fry.

Suki lunged forward onto the prairie grass as the round from Fry's Winchester whistled into the ground behind where she had stood. At the same instant Morgan wrapped her arms around Teetonka and pulled him to the ground beside her.

George flew across the empty space and lunged into Fry just as he cocked the lever and fired a second round. He tore the rifle from Fry's hands, spun him around, grabbed his wrist, and shoved it upward behind his back until the shoulder joint snapped.

Fry screamed in pain as one of the tribal cops jumped in and cuffed him. The other cop ran and picked up the 30-30.

The gunfire drove the buffalo herd into a stampede toward the far end of the large enclosure.

George glanced back at the demonstrators on the highway as they broke up and ran away. He turned and rushed to Morgan and Suki. They and the tribal members on the ground were just rising.

He held Morgan. "Are you okay?"

She nodded.

"Was anyone hit?"

"I don't think so." Morgan was wide-eyed. "How about you? Were you hurt?"

He shook his head. They both helped Suki to her feet and held her, while two of the Sioux chiefs assisted Teetonka.

Someone shouted. "One of the bulls is lying on the ground!

He may have been hit with that second shot!"

* * *

Across the enclosed area where the herd had grazed, a large older bull lay on his side. Close by, a rusty red calf stood watching him.

Morgan grabbed George's arm. "Run back to the truck and get my MedPac out of the back seat. Suki and I are going out to help him. I think he's one of the original bulls."

"What about your lock box?"

"Bring that too! I may need a sedation solution."

One of the Assiniboine tribal members opened the green metal gate for Morgan and Suki. They ran to the injured buffalo bull. The calf watched from a short distance away, then stepped back as the two of them walked around the large animal, searching for evidence of an injury or a wound from Billy Fry's second round.

Morgan knelt beside the unconscious bull and ran her fingers through the thick fur on his head. "I think I found it, Suki!"

A trickle of blood dripped from a wound near the center of its head, midway between his horns and above his eye level.

"It has to be that second shot."

Suki knelt beside Morgan. "His breathing appears to be normal. I'm going to take his vitals."

"Be careful."

George arrived with the MedPac and the lock box. "What do you need, Morgan?"

"Hand me the scissors." She reached out, waiting for George to place them in her hand, fully aware the bull could suddenly awaken and all hell would break loose. "Okay, old fellow, we're here to help you." She cut the thick hair from around the entry point of the round.

Suki said a quiet prayer as she removed the rectal thermometer from the bull. Her hands trembled. "Temperature 39 degrees centigrade, pulse rate 89, respiration 15."

Morgan called, "Suki, come help me. Take a look at this."

The round from the 30-30 had struck the animal near the center of his forehead and now protruded from the convex-shaped frontal bone surface about a centimeter.

"I think he was knocked out by the impact of the bullet hitting him at this thick critical spot on his skull during a high stress moment," Morgan said. "But I don't read permanent or critical damage. What do you think?"

"I agree," Suki said. "But we don't know how long he'll remain knocked out. We'd better anesthetize him before we do anything else."

Morgan reached in her pocket for the key chain attached to her belt and unlocked the narcotics cabinet. With George serving as their assistant, Morgan and Suki anesthetized the bull and sterilized the area around the wound. Morgan then took a pair of Webster stainless steel locking forceps with serrated jaws and extracted the bullet from the frontal bone. Blood flow was inconsequential.

Morgan handed the bullet to Suki and packed the wound. Then they waited for their patient to recover and continued monitoring his vital signs.

When the bull appeared to be stabilized, they moved a short distance away and sat on the ground. Soon after they were seated, one of the tribal policemen called to George from the fence. "I think they need a statement from me," he said. "Will the two of you be okay?"

Morgan nodded. "We're both still a bit shaken, but we'll be fine."

As George walked toward the tribal policeman, Morgan turned to Suki who sat back with her elbows on the ground observing the patient. "A penny for your thoughts."

Suki held a long blade of grass in her mouth. She leaned forward. "We've come a long way since our first meeting as scared freshmen at The University of New Mexico, haven't we?"

"Indeed we have."

"It has been an amazing journey, kiddo. And we've just begun." She grinned. "I'm glad we've begun it together."

"I am too." Morgan reached for Suki's hand and squeezed it.

They heard a grunt and stared at the bull as he whipped his tail and began to stir and quickly scrambled to their feet.

"Anesthetic is wearing off," Morgan said. She picked up the narcotics cabinet and Suki retrieved the MedPac.

"Put on your running shoes," Suki said in a low voice.

The bull grunted again. He rolled upright and stood. Morgan and Suki looked over their shoulders and quickened their pace to the gate. With his nose close to the ground, he grunted and whipped his tail. The gate opened and they walked through, greeted by handshakes and cheers. After a few moments they turned their attention back to the patient.

The bull stood watching them for a few more minutes. Then he turned and trod slowly to the herd at the far end of the pasture. The calf trotted along behind him.

George walked up behind Morgan and Suki and placed his arms around their shoulders. "That was too close a call." He shook his head. "That damned fool with the rifle. I almost lost both of you." He held them close.

"You may have saved our lives, George," Morgan said.

Suki's body gave a slight shiver. There were shadows beneath her brilliant blue eyes. "That was terrifying. Absolutely terrifying."

After a brief time they became aware of the low, deep resonance of a large drum. It was soon joined by a smaller drum; then another large one. Soon there were chants and songs. And more drums.

Surrounded by the celebrants, Suki reached into her shirt pocket and turned to Morgan. She retrieved the extracted bullet from the pocket. "You keep this, Dr. Bluestone. The patient is recovering nicely. Good job, kiddo."

Morgan grinned. "Thank you, Dr. Winters."

George looked to the west where powerful white thunderheads were forming above the ridges of the Little Rockies. "The cloud spirits are pleased."

"Shiwana," Morgan whispered.

TOM CLAFFEY

TOM CLAFFEY spent his growing-up years in northern New Mexico and southern Colorado. He majored in English literature at New Mexico Military Institute and Creighton University and, in 1954, accepted an appointment to West Point. He graduated in 1958 and became a pilot in the U.S. Air Force. In civilian life he worked in  investment securities and banking and began writing for publication in 1981. He lives in Santa Fe..